015142

MrE

ASHTEAD LIBRARY

www.surreycc.gov.uk/libraries

11/23

2

H

HY 4/10

90 09/13

COUNTY
LIBRARIES
AND LEISURE
SERVICE

Charges will be payable at the Adult rate if this item is not returned by the latest date stamped above.

L21B

SURREY
COUNTY COUNCIL

THE SECRET OF
SQUAW MOUNTAIN

By the same author

West of the Pecos
The Gold Hunters
The Gates of Hell

The Secret of Squaw Mountain

ALAN C. PORTER

A Black Horse Western

ROBERT HALE · LONDON

© Alan C. Porter 1993
First published in Great Britain 1993

ISBN 0 7090 5065 8

Robert Hale Limited
Clerkenwell House
Clerkenwell Green
London EC1R 0HT

The right of Alan C. Porter to be identified as
author of this work has been asserted by him
in accordance with the Copyright, Designs and
Patents Act 1988.

Photoset in North Wales by
Derek Doyle & Associates, Mold, Clwyd.
Printed and bound in Great Britain by
WBC Bookbinders Ltd, Bridgend, Mid-Glamorgan.

To my sons,
Simon and Andrew

ONE

The dust-laden wind rolled tumbleweed against the weathered boards of the silent buildings. Mingled with the moan of the wind, timbers creaked, loose shutters rattled on corroded hinges and doors banged fretfully. Windows shook in their frames. Only a stubborn few remained with their glass intact, the rest gaped blindly at a hostile world.

A lone rider appeared, ghost-like from the haze of ochre dust, riding an attractive, white, leopard spotted Appaloosa mare. He hunched his shoulders in a brown, alpaca coat, its collar turned up against the wind, black stetson tilted forward. A yellow bandanna swathed the rider's nose and lower face; all that could be seen, peering out from below the brim of the stetson, was a pair of hazel eyes.

Wry amusement danced in the eyes as he took in the collection of dilapidated, deserted buildings, huddled either side of a wide main street. Someone, he reflected, had shown a sense of humour. The cracked, faded signboard he had passed on the edge of town bore the name, Prosperity.

Prosperity was a dead dream. A ghost town that had been given back to nature and a bone-dry wind, with the breath of hell warming it. The choking wind blew in from the dry mesas and scrub-choked canyons that made up southern Colorado's Mesa Verde. A bleak, inhospitable land that begrudged the hand of man to tend it and fought his every turn to tame it. The town was man's try and here he had failed.

A blue-painted, flatbed wagon lay canted at an angle in the centre of the street, a front wheel off and laying in the dust next to it. The rider, Chad Hunter, gave it only a cursory glance as he swung the mare to the left. Below a peeling sign in red proclaiming 'Livery' double doors gaped open. He kneed the mare forward into the gloomy interior, relieved at being out of the wind at last. Night was only a few hours off and Prosperity offered shelter of a sort.

He swung down stiffly from the saddle, stretching and easing the kinks and cramps from his body. As he stretched, arching his back, his coat fell open to display a walnut handled Colt Frontier tied to his right leg. He pulled the bandanna from his face and tilted the stetson back, revealing the face of a man in his mid thirties, lean and handsome, tanned by the elements. A three-day growth of stubble darkened

The Secret of Squaw Mountain

his jaw and upper lip and dark, curly hair peeped from under the brim of his hat. Levis, a light blue, cotton shirt and black boots made up the rest of his dress. All were well worn, the sleeves of the coat badly patched in two places.

'Well, girl,' he addressed the mare. 'Looks like we gotta place for the night.' His eyes roamed about. Anything was better than being out in that damned wind and dust. The mare shook her head and snorted. Chad rubbed her velvet-soft muzzle and patted her sleek neck before removing the saddle and blanket and leading her into a stall. Here he slipped the harness from her head.

The stable was full of creaks, groans and rattles as the wind pummelled at the sun-dried boards of its walls. Dust flurries darted through the open entrance, whirling and eddying before collapsing into nothing.

Chad had noticed a water pump outside. He wandered out and cranked the handle a few times, causing it to squeak in protest. It was more of a gesture than anything else, so he was more than a little surprised when, with a rattle and a knock, water gushed out. The sight of it did a lot to elevate his flagging spirits. He cranked the handle again and cupped his hand under the flow. It tasted cool and sweet. He found a wooden bucket with a rope handle, half filled it and took it to the mare.

'Well, 'pears things ain't looking so bad,' he said as he watched her drink. A scout around the table revealed a second bucket. He poured a measure of oats and grain into it from the supply he carried and placed it down next to the first.

With the mare's needs catered for he took care of his own. He emptied the brackish water from his canteen, refilled it from the pump and drank long and deep. Afterwards, curiosity took him out to the wagon that he could see from the doorway. It struck him as odd to find the wagon left in such a position, abandoned in the middle of the street, almost in a hurry, to his mind. Prosperity had been deserted for a long time and the wagon didn't look that old.

His surmise turned out to be correct. There was fresh grease on the wheelless axle stub. He frowned as he looked at it. The pin had broken and it looked to have happened in the last two or three days. He wondered what had happened to the driver. It was a puzzle he did not have time to speculate on.

As the wind whirled a dust haze about him a shot rang out. Wood splinters lifted in a ragged feather on the upper edge of the wagon side nearest him as a bullet gouged the surface. He dived for the ground, heart hammering in his chest, the Colt Frontier leaping into his hand. In the split second that it happened it registered in his mind that the shot had come from a high position across the street. He crawled under the wagon to a position behind the remaining front wheel, peering through the spokes. The only place the shot could have come from was either the saloon or boarding-house across the street. The structures either side of them were single storied and did not have the elevation.

The saloon batwings waved to him. The upper windows of the saloon still boasted glass, but none were open. A section of ragged curtain blew from an open window above a sign reading 'Murphy's Boarding House' to the right of the saloon. Chad thought he detected movement at the window. The next instant the wind blew gritty dust in his eyes, forcing him to turn his head away.

A second shot sent a bullet between the spokes of the wheel to kick dust at his left elbow. He rubbed the grit from his eyes and this time was sure there was movement there. He rolled to his left, feet kicking at the sloping underside of the wagon and fired off two shots at the window, splintering the frame edge. The shots were enough to keep the sniper's head down for the few vital seconds it required for him to crawl out from under the wagon and run for the cover provided by the wooden overhang that fronted the saloon. Keeping close to the wall he moved towards the boarding-house. Glass fragments from the saloon's windows crunched underfoot, the sound whipped up and whisked away by the wind.

Dust ghosts followed his progress, whirling around his legs and slapping the ends of his three-quarter-length coat against his thighs. As he approached the end of the overhang, the window with the dirty, trailing curtain came into view overhead. He saw the end of a rifle barrel poking over the sill as the hidden sniper searched for him. Chad allowed himself a grim smile as he raised his Colt Frontier and fired. The .45 calibre bullet smashed into the underside of the sill and the rifle barrel was hurriedly withdrawn. Chad was annoyed with himself as he darted forward keeping close to the wall. He had expected to hit the barrel.

The front door of the boarding-house sagged open at the top of a short flight of steps. Chad took the steps in one leap and entered. He found himself in a small, square area. Doors led off on either side while ahead a flight of stairs led to the upper regions. Chad mounted them carefully into the gloom above. The stair boards creaked ominously beneath his feet.

At the top he found himself at the head of a narrow corridor. At the far end light spilled through a dirt encrusted window and reached out for him. A second corridor crossed the first at its centre. He moved forward through a rubble of plaster that had fallen from walls and ceiling, feet crunching noisily. At the point where the corridors crossed he paused and peered cautiously left and right. Doors led off on either side. Some were open, providing welcome patches of light.

Rattles and thumps filled the crumbling building with spectral noises. From the outside position of the window used by the hidden sniper,

The Secret of Squaw Mountain

Chad's target lay behind the first door to the right. He moved into the middle of the corridor and stole forward. The door he headed for was closed. He was almost upon it when the floor beneath his right foot gave way with a splintering crash. There was little he could do to save himself. His left leg folded under him while his right leg plunged to the hip, only a rafter beneath that he painfully straddled, saving him from a long fall. The gun flew from his grasp as he put his hands down to steady himself, slithering out of reach. Wedged thus, the rafter digging into his crotch, he was aware of the door opening and light spilling out over him.

'Don't try anything, mister, or you're dead,' a female voice warned. Chad jerked his head up and found himself looking down the barrel of a Winchester, clasped in a pair of slim hands. Chad's eyes were only partly on the weapon. The centre of his attention was focused on the tense, pretty face above it.

Chestnut hair flowed about her head and fell to slim shoulders in a glorious, rich brown cascade. She wore levis and boots and a white shirt that did little to hide the generous curves of her body. She looked to be in her early twenties and eyes, big and doe-like, observed him frostily. Her mouth was a thin, angry line beneath a button nose.

'Evening, ma'am.' He gave his most disarming smile displaying white, even teeth.

'Who are you?' she demanded brusquely.

'The one you're shooting at and mighty puzzled as to why.'

'You're one of McMurdo's men,' she barked decisively, expression hard and unrelenting.

'Do you mind if'n I climb outta this hole, ma'am? It's proving a mite uncomfortable on the leg, not to mention other parts.'

A hard smile touched her lips.

'Make a move, mister and you won't have any other parts to mention,' she promised darkly.

'Now hold on lady and back off,' Chad snapped. 'You were shooting at me, remember, and I've never heard of any McMurdo.'

She shook her head.

'Only McMurdo's men would be in Prosperity,' she persisted doggedly.

'Wrong, ma'am. McMurdo's men, you and me. The name's Chad Hunter and I'm just looking for a place to bed down for the night. Now, whether you like it or not, I'm getting out of this hole.' So saying he ignored her and set to freeing his leg. It proved a painful struggle, but finally he was on his feet, back to the wall opposite her. He raised his hands, palms outwards, to shoulder level in a gesture to show that he was not armed.

'What are you doing in Prosperity?' she asked.

'You mean other than being used as target practice by you and falling through rotten floors?' He managed a tight smile. 'Just passing through on my way to Grand Mesa. Dust storm kinda blew me off course and here I am. I don't know what

The Secret of Squaw Mountain

your beef is with this McMurdo character, but don't lay it on me.' He fixed his gaze on her and saw a flicker of uncertainty leap into her eyes.

'Maybe I was wrong,' she admitted hesitantly.

'I'll allow that's the first bit o' good sense I've heard,' he said.

'I only said, maybe,' she pointed out stiffly.

'Cora! What's happening out there?' a voice called from within the room, a male voice. The girl half turned her head.

'Found a man sneaking about, Pa. Ow!' The last word flew startled from her lips as Chad saw his chance in her momentary distraction. He stepped over the hole and twisted the rifle from her grip and then retrieved his gun, returning it to its holster.

'I wasn't sneaking about,' Chad corrected, backing the girl into the room and peering around. In one corner an elderly man in a grubby white suit lay on a pile of blankets. His right pants leg was torn from ankle to knee revealing a lower leg swathed in a bloodstained cloth. The man had propped himself up on his elbows, face grey with pain. A tangle of white hair fell untidily about his head and clawed at his eyes.

Chad eyed the two in wonderment.

'What happened to him?'

'Took a bullet in the leg,' she said sullenly. 'But then you'd know that.'

Chad sighed.

'Dammit, girl. I'm not here to harm you or your

pa. Here.' Into her surprised hands he thrust the rifle. 'I'll help him if'n I can.' He turned his back on her and moved across to the man, who appeared to be in his early sixties. The girl followed after a second's hesitation.

'You know about bullet wounds?' she asked as he gently removed the makeshift bandage.

'Sure as hell have to with women like you about,' he retorted sharply. He didn't see the face she pulled at his back in return as he examined the wound. The bullet was still lodged in the calf. It must have been near spent by the time it had hit the old man.

'The name is Wellbeloved, young man. Professor Jonas Wellbeloved, from Seattle,' the old man introduced himself with a touch of pride and Chad grinned.

'Sure is a mouthful to chew on, Professor,' he remarked.

'My daughter, Cora, you have already met.'

'That's for sure,' Chad agreed, sitting back on his haunches. 'Chad Hunter.' He threw the girl a half smile before returning his gaze to the professor. 'Professor eh. Never met a professor afore,' he mused.

'I'm an archaeologist. I study ...'

'The past through bones and bits left behind,' Chad interrupted and at the surprised look that entered the professor's eyes, added, 'We aren't all dumb cowpokes, Professor. 'Sides, I once dallied with a school-marm out Topeka way. She learned me a thing or two.'

For the first time in days the old man chuckled.

'I bet she did, Mr Hunter. What about the leg?'

'The bullet needs to come out and the wound cleaned. It's starting to get poisoned. Leave it much longer and you'll be hopping about on one leg 'stead o' two. Either that or you'll be dead.' His frank words brought a gasp from the girl. The old man eyed him ruefully.

'You don't pull your punches do you, Mr Hunter?'

'I speak as I see it, Professor, that's why I'm allowing you'll forgive me now.' With that and as a puzzled frown began to form on the professor's face, Chad's right hand shot out. The clenched fist caught the unsuspecting man on the point of the chin with a solid smack and laid him out without a cry.

After a shocked, stunned silence from the girl that lasted only a few seconds, she swung the rifle up to cover him, eyes blazing.

'You are from McMurdo,' she accused bitterly and her finger began to tighten on the trigger.

TWO

Alarm showed in Chad's face. On his knees at the side of the old man he lifted his hands.

'Settle down, girl, and don't go pulling on that fool trigger. Like as not your pa won't last another day or so less'n that bullet's took out. Best he sleeps while I do it. Now make yourself useful. I'll need water from the pump. You'll find a bucket in the livery by my mare. Poke about in my saddle-bags over there and you'll find a bottle of whiskey. Bring 'em here as fast as you can.'

'Now wait a minute ...' she began.

'Ain't gotta minute. Your pa won't be out long and I'd like to be finished by the time he wakes and I reckon he'd like it even more.'

'Do you know what you're doing?'

'Enough. Now git!'

She eyed him hesitantly, then with a final distressed glance at her unconscious pa, fled from the room. In the five minutes it took her to gather his requirements, the deed was done.

Chad had worked quickly. The bullet had

almost passed through the calf and it had been relatively easy to cut in from the opposite side and extract it. She almost fainted at the amount of blood that had pooled on the floor and his scarlet hands. A whimper fell from her lips in a sudden chalk-white face.

'Rags, girl, and something to use as a bandage,' he ordered roughly as he took the water and whiskey from her, setting them on the floor by his side. In her absence he had rolled the old man onto his stomach in order to work on the calf more easily. He rinsed his hands in the water and waited impatiently as she rummaged in a carpet-bag in one corner and returned with a white cotton blouse, tearing it into strips.

After drying his hands he took a cartridge from his belt and used his teeth to draw the bullet from the shell. She watched silently as he poured the gunpowder into the wound. He ordered her to look away as he struck a match and touched it to the gunpowder. There was a hiss and a flare that he saw through his own closed lids. A tiny jet of flame lanced through the newly-made exit in the calf. Flesh sizzled briefly as the flame cauterized the wound and filled the air with its acrid taint.

With the bleeding reduced to a slow seep, Chad cleaned the wound and poured a measure of whiskey over it. Using some squares of cloth as pads, that she held in place, Chad bandaged the wound with a strip of cloth. When he had finished he gently turned the old man over onto his back and supported the leg, under the knee, with a rolled up blanket. He rinsed his hands again in the bucket, dried them on a scrap of cloth that remained and arose on creaking knees, taking a stiff pull at the bottle before setting it down at the old man's side.

'Will he be all right?' She spoke tremulously for the first time in what seemed an age, her throat dry and raspy.

'Time will tell, girl,' Chad answered as he rubbed a layer of sweat from his brow. 'I figure Grand Mesa to be half a day's ride to the west. We'll let him rest up for the night then head out in the morning. Reckon I can fix the wagon and my mare can pull it. Best let a doctor take a look at that leg to make sure.'

'If McMurdo's men let us leave,' she said dolefully. 'It was them that shot Pa, took our horses and left us here, only they don't leave us for long. They keep coming back, making sure we don't leave.' Tears sprang into her eyes. 'They won't be satisfied until we're dead and I don't know why.' Her voice broke as the tension within her drained away. She turned her back on him to hide the flood of hot tears that rolled down her dusty cheeks.

Chad felt a wave of protectiveness wash through him. He never could stand to see a woman cry. He reached out awkwardly and gripped her shaking shoulders. The touch was enough to turn her into him and push her weeping face into his chest. He could feel her body convulsing against his and a great flush of anger against a group of men he had never seen rolled hotly over him. He held her loosely to him until finally she broke away, eyes red, face flushed with embarrassment.

'I'm s...sorry, Mr Hunter. Stupid female reaction.' She dabbed at her eyes.

'Don't worry, ma'am, please,' Chad broke in hastily. 'The name's Chad. Now why don't you tell me who these characters are.'

'I'm surprised you didn't run into them.'

'People don't ride in dust storms less'n they have to. Guess they weren't riding today.' He shrugged.

There were a few ramshackle chairs in the room. She sat on one and stared broodingly at a point on the floor.

'The who part is easy enough. They work for Sam McMurdo who bosses the EM Mining Company at Squaw Mountain.' She paused and eyed him brightly. 'Please call me Cora.'

'You don't know why they're after you, Cora?' Chad prompted, wandering across to the window. It seemed to him that the wind had dropped a tad. He turned and leaned back against the wall, thumbs hooked in his gunbelt.

'I can't think of any reason, unless it was because of the man.'

'Man?' Chad frowned.

'Pa and I were camped in a canyon at the base of

Squaw Mountain. For years Pa's been chasing a tribe of Indians that died out some five hundred years ago. The Anasazi. Have you ever heard of them, Chad?'

'Don't recollect that I have.' Chad shook his head.

'According to the Navaho it means the Ancient Ones. Pa can tell you more about them than I. Anyway it was on our third night at the canyon when this man staggered into our camp. He was in a terrible state. He looked to have had no food or water for days and his body was criss-crossed with scars. A lot were old, but some were new. Pa said the scars were whip marks.' She shuddered.

'Go on,' Chad prompted.

'We did what we could to make the man comfortable, but he died an hour later without saying a word. He never spoke at all so we never knew who he was or where he had come from. It was a short while later that Garth Corday rode into our camp with a bunch of his ruffians.'

'Corday being the gent that comes here?'

'Corday is head of security at the mine. It's a gold mine and pretty rich, so they say. McMurdo has Corday and his men on the payroll to keep law and order in the area, although there's very little law where Corday is concerned. He said the man was wanted for stealing gold from the mine and wanted to know what he had told us. He didn't believe it when we said nothing. Practically accused us of lying.' She flicked a strand of hair from her eyes. 'He got quite abusive about it. In the end they left and took the body with them. Pa was quite annoyed about it and insisted that he would be seeing McMurdo the following morning to complain about Corday's behaviour.' She paused, looking down at the unconscious man.

'And did he?' Chad asked.

'There was no need. McMurdo turned up at our camp the very next morning along with Corday. He told us we were trespassing on EM property and to get out immediately or steps would be taken to have us removed. The whole thing was so ludicrous because it was McMurdo who gave us permission to be there in the first place.' She shrugged helplessly.

'Did he give a reason for his change of mind?'

'Said the area was earmarked for stage two mining development, whatever that is, said the area was out of bounds and thought that we were five miles further along. He lied, Chad. He knew exactly where we were. Pa had shown it to him on the map before we even moved into the canyon.'

'But you moved anyway?'

'We had little choice. Move or be moved. McMurdo was so anxious for us to move that we only had time to grab a few things. The tent is still there as far as I know. Anyway, Corday and his men were sent to make sure we kept moving. They trailed us to Properity and then tried to kill us.' A look of horror filled her eyes.

'And that's when the professor took a bullet?'

Chad said, by now intrigued. 'This Corday fella. What's he look like?'

'Horrible. Big man. Smiles a lot. Blond hair. I guess some women would find him attractive. You know him?'

'Name seems familiar,' Chad said noncommittally, but inside he was churning as distant memories from the past stirred. 'Go on with what you were saying.'

'There's not much else to tell. They chased us into Prosperity and the wagon lost a wheel. I managed to get Pa up here. They didn't try too hard to get us out. They took the horse and left us stranded. They come back each day and so far I've managed to hold them off, but they seem to be in no hurry. It's almost as if it's a game to them.'

A cold smile curved Chad's lips, but never reached his eyes. If this Corday was who he thought it was, then that would be just about right.

'No need to hurry. You and your pa are not going anywhere. They have you where they want you. Once you run out of bullets that will be it.'

'I almost have,' she admitted. 'Just one left. I used the rest on you. I haven't apologized yet for mistaking you for one of McMurdo's men. I'm sorry, Chad.'

'Pay it no heed, Cora. In your shoes I'd've been even more jittery.' Chad felt admiration for the girl. 'And you reckon all that's happened is down to this dead man?'

'Or what they thought he might have said before he died.' She shook her head dismally. 'The trouble is that now you are trapped along with us.'

A bleak smile played about his stubbled lips.

'That remains to be seen,' he replied. Further conversation was cut short by the old man groaning as consciousness returned.

'The Anasazi, Chad. The Ancient Ones!' Professor Jonas Wellbeloved's eyes gleamed in the glow of a single lantern. Night had long since fallen and the wind had died away. Prosperity lay silent under the frosty stars. He sat propped up against the wall, fortified more by the whiskey, that had pinched colour into his thin cheeks, rather than the food Chad had prepared earlier. The whiskey had deadened the pain from his injured leg and Cora thought he looked better, more his old self. She sat at his side while Chad occupied a creaking chair facing them. The lantern sat on the floor between them. 'They disappeared in the thirteenth century leaving behind a legacy of a culture so far advanced for a primitive people, that it has not been surpassed to this day.

'They had cities, huge cities made of stone and built long, straight roads between them. They traded with the plains Indians, then something happened in the twelfth century. The Anasazi civilisation went into decline. Almost overnight they deserted their cities and spread out across the continent and established new settlements, this time settling in canyons and building their cities in the canyon walls.'

'Like the Pueblo Indians,' Chad said.

'And the Hopis. There are a number of tribes that can trace their ancestors back to the Anasazi when they ceased being a nation of their own and became absorbed into others.'

'Where did they come from, Professor?'

'New Mexico. Their next famous canyon city was found in Chaco Canyon, but I believe another lies somewhere in the canyons of the Mesa Verde. I have followed vague references to the Anasazi for years. The latest led me to the canyon at Squaw Mountain. It was there Cora and I found a cave.' Excitement grew in the professor's slurring voice as he mixed words and whiskey. 'In that cave were wall paintings that proved my theory that the Anasazi had settled in Mesa Verde. I never finished deciphering the paintings before McMurdo and his ruffians had us thrown out. But I did decipher enough to know that a group of Anasazi went up onto Squaw Mountain and that's where I must go next.' He hiccoughed and leaned the back of his head against the wall. 'I've got to know the secret of Squaw Mountain,' he muttered as he lifted the near empty whiskey bottle to his lips only to have his hand stopped by Cora.

'I think you're numb enough now, Pa,' she said and took the bottle from him.

'It is for medicinal purposes,' he pointed out, eyes following its departure with disappointment.

'Then that's what we'll keep the rest for,' she replied crisply and Chad couldn't keep himself from laughing at the man's crestfallen look.

'There was one part of the wall paintings that was very strange. As far as I could tell, it was a warning for anyone venturing onto the mountain, to beware of He-with-no-Voice.' The professor shrugged. 'Some Indian legend to frighten the superstitious I suppose.' He shrugged again.

'You seem to have forgotten that Squaw Mountain is owned by the mining company,' Cora pointed out. 'McMurdo's certainly not going to let you into it.'

'Then we'll go to a higher authority. McMurdo runs the mine, he doesn't own it,' the professor said. 'And Chad will help us, won't you, Chad?'

'Pa!' Cora gave Chad an embarrassed glance. 'I'm sure Mr Hunter has plans of his own?'

'We'll wait and see what the doctor says after he's taken a look at that leg,' Chad drawled with a smile.

'You both seem to be overlooking McMurdo's men. They may not be so inclined to let us ride out of here,' she pointed out tartly.

'That's a point,' the professor agreed glumly. 'What do we do, Chad?'

They both eyed him expectantly.

'Get some sleep. Tomorrow's going to be a long day,' he said in a leisurely fashion and arose from the chair.

* * *

The four riders rode into Prosperity with the rising sun. In the lead Garth Corday smiled. He always smiled, a wide, expansive smile that exuded friendliness and charm, but it was only by looking into his blue eyes that the real Garth Corday could be glimpsed. The smile and the friendliness never touched the eyes. They were as cold and unfeeling as ice.

He was a big man, wide shoulders clad in a light tan coat, a brown stetson on his close cut, blond hair. He rode with ease and confidence, without a care in the world, a pearl handled Navy Colt on his left hip. Behind him three men rode in a line across the street. Two were clad in nondescript range clothes, hard-eyed, unsmiling men. The third had the touch of hell about him.

Clad entirely in black including fine leather gloves, he was thin and mean looking. His dark, high-cheekboned face could have been Mexican, could have been Indian, maybe a mixture of both with perhaps negro in his ancestry. 'Indios' as he was called, did not know and did not care. He looked more Indian at the moment with a blood-red headband tied about his head to keep his long, black hair from his face. He said very little, ready to let the twin ebony-handled Smith and Wessons on his hips do the talking for him.

The other two wore silver stars pinned to their shirts that from a distance could have had them mistaken for lawmen. On closer inspection the stars bore the inscription, 'EM Mining. Security' in a circle. Indios would not wear one and Corday did not need to.

Harness buckles jingled and leather creaked, merging with the measured thudding of slow-moving horses. Corday was bored with his 'game', the old man and the girl would die today. He would let Indios have the girl. It would be entertainment for them all.

'Wake up, girl, it's playtime,' Corday yelled. He had reined in his sorrel in the middle of the street before the boarding-house and leisurely hooked a knee about the pommel of his saddle, the smile wide on his lips. 'Either you come out or we come in and get you. Don' mind which.'

Cora stood to one side of the window, hardly daring to breathe as she listened. The professor was on his feet using the back of a chair to take the weight off his injured leg. Of Chad there was no sign. He had taken himself off to sleep in the livery overnight and not returned. A feeling of panic touched her. Maybe he had rode on in the night and left them to the tender mercies of McMurdo's men. The mind-numbing thought was dismissed by a voice from below.

'Mr Corday, there's a horse in the livery.' It was one of the badge wearers. A wicker from the Appaloosa had reached his ears and he had peeled from the group and dismounted in the livery entrance. 'Ain't no one about. Saddle's on the floor.' The man took his lariat and disappeared inside. He reappeared a few moments later dragging the reluctant Appaloosa at the end of a rope. 'She's a fine beast, Mr Corday.'

'Got company have we?' Corday shouted up in the window. 'Well that surely is fine and dandy.' The smile that had faltered on finding the horse returned, but a tension now charged his body. He unhooked his leg as he spoke and slid the toe of his boot into the stirrup.

'Stealing a man's horse is a shooting offence, hombre.' The mildly uttered words had all heads snapping in the direction of the voice. Chad Hunter had appeared in the street and was slowly walking towards Corday. In Chad's left hand he held a shotgun, the barrels cut down and angled at the sky, the stock resting on his hip. His right hand hung loose and ready by the Colt Frontier.

Corday recovered from his surprise quickly.

'Stealing? No sir,' he replied cordially. 'Just admiring a mighty fine animal. Garth Corday, sir, and who might I have the pleasure of addressing?'

Chad gave no outward sign of the turmoil that was churning his insides. The man's name had stirred memories when he had first heard it. Seeing the man had brought the ten-year-old memories to the surface. The smiling man on the sorrel was none other than the 'Butcher of Abilene'.

THREE

'Just a stranger passing through a dead town,' Chad replied, his confidence bolstered by the feel of the shotgun and the fact that three of the men were still mounted and in plain view. The fourth man was partially obscured by the Appaloosa. 'Folks have called me a lot of names in my time, but I answer best to Chad Hunter.' Chad had not missed the black clad rider. The man exuded an aura of death. He was a professional killer and of the four the one to watch.

'Well, Chad,' Corday blustered genially, keeping a wary eye on the shotgun. He knew the devastation they could cause at close quarters. 'Ain't no need for guns. We're peaceable men on company business.'

Chad came to a halt a few yards from Corday, eyeing the smiling man without expression.

'That being the case, you won't need yours,' Chad pointed out, matching Corday's amiable air. 'I'd be obliged for you and your boys to drop your guns into the dust.'

'I said we're peaceable, friend ...'

'But I'm not, friend,' Chad hissed and suddenly there was winter in his eyes and voice. 'And my finger's getting awful twitchy. All you've gotta remember, before your boy in black plays at being hero, that if anything happens to me you won't be around to enjoy it.' He could see that the meaning was not lost on Corday. The man's veneer of the friendly, helpful cowboy slipped a little. Indios might just forget that the gun was not pointing at him and make a play.

'No gunplay, boys,' he warned. 'Now, Chad ...' Corday began, but Chad cut him off.

'Time's running out, Corday, and so is my patience.' Gone was the bland, quiet cowboy that Cora knew. In his place a man as hard and mean as the black clad man that rode with Corday. From the upper window Cora had heard the interplay of words with trepidation, now that feeling changed to one of awe as she watched the four toss their guns down. Corday's face was now as sullen as his men's, the irritating smile gone. 'You and your pa can come on out, Cora,' Chad called. He smiled at Corday. 'Best you dismount, gents, and form a line. There's a wagon to be fixed.'

'You're making a terrible mistake, friend,' Corday grated through clenched teeth.

'Doing that all the time,' Chad replied evenly. 'Kinda makes life interesting.'

'It also makes life short.'

The Secret of Squaw Mountain

By the time Cora and the professor had emerged, the latter supporting himself with Cora's rifle, the task of fixing the wagon had begun. It was a job for brawn rather than brains. While the two badge wearers lifted the corner of the wagon, Corday and Indios manhandled the wheel back onto the axle. Chad had found a new pin in the livery to replace the broken one. Using the badge wearers, Chad had them unsaddle Corday's sorrel and, to the man's obvious anger, hitch it between the shafts of the wagon. In the meantime Chad had sent Cora to the pump to fetch a bucket of water.

'I'll surely remember your words about stealing another man's horse,' Corday ground out.

'Seems to me that a horse pulled this wagon here and left with you after your first visit. 'Sides I'm only borrowing old red here. You can pick him up again in the livery at Grand Mesa.'

Cora came stumbling from the pump outside the livery, water slopping from a bucket. She had no idea what this was for until Chad had her collect up the discarded handguns.

'You can't do this, Hunter,' Corday snarled, knowing what Chad planned to do. 'That gun was handmade ...'

'Drop them in the bucket,' Chad said to Cora. Indios watched dispassionately as his treasured Smith and Wessons sank in the bucket.

Just before the three were ready to leave Chad collected their rifles and threw them in the back of the wagon while the badge wearers unsaddled the three remaining horses and dumped the saddles in a heap in the middle of the street. Chad fired his handgun beneath the feet of the horses and they galloped away in fright. This done he swung astride his own horse, that he had had one of the men saddle.

'You can pick your rifles up at the sheriff's office in Grand Mesa. Shouldn't take too long rounding up your horses.' It was at this point that Indios uttered his first words.

'You are a dead man, señor,' he said quietly. There was no rancour or malice in the voice or anger in the face. Just a flat calmness.

'We all are, friend.' Chad said mildly. 'It's just a matter of when we lie down. How do they call you?'

'Indios.' It was the Mexican word for Indian.

Chad eyed him. 'Adios amigo.'

'We will meet again,' Indios called after him as he rode, alongside the wagon, out of the dead, forgotten town.

'We beat them, Chad, we beat them!' The professor was jubilant. He sat in the rear of the wagon on a makeshift bed. 'We'll see just what the authorities have to say in Grand Mesa.' Chad said nothing to disillusion the old man. If the missing company was important to the town, the town would not be eager to stir up trouble.

Prosperity was a tiny jumble of buildings on the horizon when Cora asked. 'Will they come after us when they've caught their horses, Chad?'

The Secret of Squaw Mountain 35

'No need. They know where we're going.' He seemed remarkably unconcerned.

'Was it wise to tell them?' she asked.

'Ain't but one place to head for in this direction, but Grand Mesa. 'Sides, do you want me branded a horse thief? Corday knows where to pick up his horse and rifles.'

They rode in silence. To the north rose the San Juan mountains, snow dominating their ragged peaks beneath the harsh blue of the sky.

'You seem to know Corday from somewhere.' They had stopped to spell the horses and give the professor a rest from the jolting wagon. Chad had made coffee and stood by the wagon, looking back in the direction of the now invisible Prosperity, sipping the black, scalding brew.

'Heard of him. Ten years ago he was the sheriff of Abilene, brought in by the good folks of that town to clean the place up, get rid of the unwanted element that was making their lives a misery. He did it all right, but what the good folks of Abilene didn't realize was that they were swapping one hell with another. Corday works in a particular style. He builds up an army of gunmen all around him and proceeds to take over the town and storekeepers suddenly find they have to pay a levy to the sheriff to keep their stores from being broken into.' Chad paused to sip at his mug.

'And the townsfolk paid him?' Cora asked.

'Had no choice. Corday had 'em over a barrel. Pay up or he'd give the town back to the outlaws and roughnecks.'

'They let him get away with it?' Cora sounded incredulous.

'With a bunch of gunmen and killers like that Indios fella to back him up, Corday could get away with anything. But it was the other side of his nature that gave him his nickname. Anyone that ended up in Corday's jail came out of it a lot worse off than they went in. Some even came out in a pine box. Corday liked to torture his prisoners. He called it interrogation in the pursuance of the law.' Chad paused to drink again from the mug.

'You said he had a nickname?' Cora prompted and Chad smiled bleakly.

'They called him the Butcher of Abilene. Stories say that the nights were never free from the screams of prisoners coming from the jail, but then these stories tend to get added to. But there's no doubt that Corday was as crooked as the men he was employed to get rid of. He began to demand more money from the people and finally a group got together and hired a gunfighter to get rid of him. A fella known as the Undertaker. Corday got wind of it and sent his men out to lay an ambush for this Undertaker fella.' Chad emptied the dregs from his mug.

'Why did he get named the Undertaker?'

'They reckon that anyone who faced him never lived to walk away.'

Cora shivered. 'Sounds like they were made for each other. The Undertaker and the Butcher of

Abilene. What happened next? I take it the Undertaker lost his claim as Corday is still here?'

'No ma'am.' Chad allowed himself a smile. 'Corday underestimated this Undertaker fella, 'pears he had a mite more about him than Corday reckoned. The six fellas Corday sent out came back tied to their horses, dead. One had a note pinned to him to say he'd be in directly to take care of Corday. Corday didn't stay around. He hightailed out of there and that was the last folks around Abilene heard of him.'

'What about the Undertaker? What happened to him?' Cora asked.

'He vanished as well.' Chad shrugged. 'With Corday gone there was nothing left for him to do. I guess his job was done, he'd got rid of Corday from Abilene so that was it.'

'You never saw Corday yourself, Chad?' the professor asked.

'I was in Abilene just after it happened and the local newspaper was full o' the story. Ran it with a big likeness of Corday on the front page. Looks like he's back in the same sort of business again, under the banner of the EM Mining Company.'

'If he is the same man then you had better watch your back,' the professor said grimly.

'I intend to,' Chad replied. 'Which brings me to the point that once we reach Grand Mesa, we should part company. With Corday and his boys on the prod, I may not be too healthy to be around.'

'In that case it may be healthier to stay together. Safety in numbers and all that,' the professor pointed out as Chad kicked dust over the small fire he had built to make the coffee.

'You got business in Grand Mesa, Chad?' Cora asked as they continued their journey. 'You said that's where you were headed before the storm took you into Prosperity.'

'Meeting my brother Tom there. We keep in touch and try to meet up once a year. Business took him to Grand Mesa. I was in Durango getting ready to head out for Tucson, so Grand Mesa suited me just fine, being on the way, so to speak. Speaking of which, we'd best be on our way, folks.'

After Prosperity, that had risen from the arid dust with only tumbleweed and dry scrub for company, Grand Mesa proved a welcome contrast. The terrain had gradually grown more fertile as their journey progressed. Grass appeared, hesitantly at first, in tired clumps then in a vast prairie of waving green. Stands of trees, oak and elm appeared, then Grand Mesa itself, with the snow-capped bulk of Squaw Mountain dominating the northern horizon. It was to the rivers that tumbled from the mountain that the region owed its fertility.

Grand Mesa was a hustling, bustling town of stone and wood buildings, covered sidewalks and gaudy store fronts. The wide main street, that ran a north/south line, was busy with heavy, lumbering freight wagons. The stage from Durango had not long since pulled in to add a sort of chaos to the busy scene as people gathered outside the stage depot for parcels or letters they were expecting. Numerous side streets radiated from the main street, leading into quieter, residential areas.

On the way into town they paused at a house with a white picket fence and a doctor's shingle outside. Doc Forbes took a look at the professor's leg, and declared there was nothing more he could do than what had already been done. The leg would heal fine if the professor kept off it for a week and let nature take its course. He charged them two bits for his time and sent them on their way.

With the professor and Cora installed in a small boarding-house sandwiched between the bank and the general store, Chad took the wagon to the livery stable. The livery man's eyes popped when he saw and recognized the sorrel. He also recognized the wagon that the professor had hired from him. The man eyed him suspiciously.

'Don't know you, mister, but that ain't the horse that went with that wagon and you ain't the one that hired the wagon in the first place. Sorrel belongs to Mr Corday at the mine. Ain't no shaft-bred animal.' With hands on hips he eyed Chad from beneath a fall of dark hair.

'I can see you're a very perceptive man,' Chad intoned. 'Everythin' you said is right. I'd be right pleased if'n you carried on doing things right and that is curry and feed the animal. This Corday fella'll be along directly to get him and if'n he ain't looking groomed and happy, old Garth is not going to take too kindly to you.'

The man's belligerence fled. People that got on the wrong end of Garth Corday's temper lived to regret it.

'What about mah horse? The one that went out with the wagon?'

'See Corday,' Chad called back over his shoulder as he walked away carrying the rifles from the wagon.

Sheriff Roy Cooper enjoyed the quiet life. Apart from the occasional saloon ruckus, Grand Mesa was fairly peaceful, except for now. What the man called Chad Hunter was telling him did not make for a peaceful future. He listened slack-jawed from his chair, smoothing a drooping moustache with the thumb and forefinger of his left hand.

'So, Sheriff, what are you going to do about Corday and his men?' Chad concluded.

'Do, mister?' Roy's face now wore a haggard, uneasy look. 'I'm gonna give you a bit of advice. Get the hell outta Grand Mesa afore Corday catches up with you.'

'Sheriff, the professor and his daughter are the injured party. If I hadn't happened along they'd be dead by now.'

'Mister, I've only got your word for that. Happen Garth Corday can provide a dozen witnesses to

The Secret of Squaw Mountain 41

say you and the professor are damn liars.' Roy leaned forward on his desk.

'So you're not going to do anything?'

'There ain't nothin' to do unless Mr Corday decides to press charges against you and those other folks for trespassing on EM land. Prosperity belongs to the mining company and so does half of Grand Mesa. Make it easy on yourself, mister, leave now and we can all die of old age.'

Chad left the sheriff's office and returned to the boarding-house. The sheriff's reaction was no more or less than he had expected.

'It's scandalous,' the professor declared indignantly from his bed where he was resting his leg. 'We'll soon see about this. I'm not without some influence.'

'In Seattle, maybe. Grand Mesa's a long way from your sort of civilisation, closer to what you study. Unless you ranch or mine the law ain't interested in what happens to you.'

'Nevertheless I shall send a few telegrams,' he insisted.

'As you wish, Professor. Me, I'm gonna get me a bath and shave and then take a look for Tom. Gotta year's catching up to do.'

Grand Mesa boasted three boarding-houses and two hotels. After his bath and shave and a fresh change of clothes, Chad went about the task of checking each one until he found his brother or could leave a message if his brother was not there. It was in the Mesa Hotel that Chad found what he wanted and something he didn't want.

'So finally someone's turned up.' The thin, balding reception clerk had a sneering manner that Chad found instantly annoying. 'Five days' rent is what's owed on that room and that's what it'll cost if'n he wants his things back.'

'Hold on, fella,' Chad protested sharply. 'How about you run that by me again?'

The clerk sighed and rubbed a tomahawk nose.

'Tom Hunter booked in here five days ago. He spent one night and the following day rode out and ain't ever come back. I've been turning clients away 'cause of that.' He glared at Chad.

'Damn your clients, mister,' Chad said abruptly, stepping forward and crashing both clenched hands down onto the counter top. The clerk took a hurried step back, colour draining from his face. 'Have you reported his disappearance to the sheriff?'

'Mister, drifters come and ...' The man ended with a startled, terrified squawk as Chad leaned across the counter, grabbed a handful of vest front and hauled the man forward.

'I'm getting real short on patience, fella. My brother was no drifter. Now you'd better start thinking and thinking real hard. I want to know where my brother was going that day and I hope for your sake that the answer is not, "I don't know"?'

The clerk's mouth gaped like a stranded fish and finally words came out.

'He just said he was going to the mine and that he'd be back later, only he didn't. Please, mister, you're hurting me.'

'That's good, 'cause while you're still hurting you aren't dead,' Chad replied. 'Anything else?'

'That was all, I swear.'

'Then I suggest we go up to his room.' Chad released his grip. 'Don't worry, you'll get your money, but just for now that room stays as it is.'

Left alone in the room Chad went through his brother's belongings. It was at the bottom of a carpet-bag that Chad happened on the notebook. Tom had used it in diary form, dating each entry. The last entry was dated five days ago.

Seen McMurdo. Get the feeling that he's hiding something. Don't like the man, nor his head of security, Corday. I shall investigate the mine tomorrow to try and find out how less workers means increased output.

Chad closed the notebook with a puzzled frown at its contents that soon slipped into bleaker thoughts as he left the room. He was getting a bad feeling inside.

FOUR

'Well, the answer's quite plain to me,' the professor announced after Chad had returned to the boarding-house, puzzling over the entry in the book.

'It is?' Chad gave the professor an admiring look.

'Less workers and increased output means that McMurdo is not paying his workers. That can only mean slave labour!' The professor snapped the book shut and handed it back to Chad.

'The man that came into our camp, Pa,' Cora put in excitedly. She was now wearing a simple floral cotton dress after bathing the trail dust away. That and her subtle perfume formed an appealing attraction to Chad.

'The whip marks,' the professor mused. 'And the man's hands certainly showed heavy callousing.' The light of understanding dawned in his eyes. 'That would explain McMurdo's reason for turning us off the site.'

'It would also make sense of why Corday

wanted you both dead,' Chad pointed out grimly. 'They were afraid the man might have told you what was going on at the mine.'

'Where does your brother Tom fit into all this, Chad?' Cora asked after they had taken a moment to digest the unpleasant news.

'Tom's a mining inspector. Travels around the big mining concerns making sure the mines are being maintained properly and corners are not being cut. I think it's time I had a chat with this McMurdo fella.' There was a grim note to his voice. Cora followed him out of the room and onto the landing, catching his arm before he descended the stairs.

'Take care, Chad,' she said anxiously, then reddened and released his arm, embarrassed by her sudden concern that she was aware was not just out of friendship. The thought made her blush deepen.

As he clattered down the stairs Chad found that he liked being worried over.

Chad made his way down the street to the offices of the EM Mining Company that he had spotted earlier next to the bank. It was late afternoon and the business premises were beginning to close for the day. The door of the EM Mining Company yielded to his touch and he found himself in a small reception area that reminded him of a cathouse in Topeka he had once visited. A plush russet carpet ran from wall to wall and dotted about were potted plants. In the sunlight that sprayed through the window, the light, wood panelled walls seemed to glow. An elderly woman, seated at a desk angled in one corner, glanced up as he entered and registered disapproval on her pinched features.

'Yes?' she said abruptly. 'We are just closing ...'

'You go on and close, ma'am. McMurdo about?'

'MR McMurdo is in conference and can see no one.' Her eyes flickered to a rust-coloured door facing the street entrance. Chad noticed the involuntary glance. 'Have you an appointment? Mr McMurdo sees no one without an appointment.'

'He'll see me, ma'am,' Chad stated as he headed for the door. The woman sprang to her feet in alarm.

'You can't go in there,' her voice shrilled.

Samuel Horace McMurdo looked up from a large ebony desk as the door flew open. His fat, heavy-jowled features showed surprise and annoyance at being disturbed. He was bald except for a small area above each ear. He fixed Chad with a glare, but Chad was not looking at him, but at the man that McMurdo had been in 'conference' with.

A smile broke across Chad's face.

'Howdy again, Garth,' he greeted cheerfully. 'Thanks for the loan of the horse, it was sure appreciated. It's over in the livery waiting for you to claim and the sheriff's looking after your rifles.'

Corday's mouth fell open.

'You!'

'You know his man, Corday?'

'It's the one I was telling you about,' Corday said.

'I'm sorry, Mr McMurdo.' The woman from outside appeared at Chad's elbow. 'He pushed through before I could stop him.'

'That's all right, Miss Jackson. Leave us,' McMurdo growled and leaned back in his seat eyeing Chad, hands clasped across his ample stomach that strained the seams of a grey vest matching the grey suit he wore. He waited until the door had closed before saying, 'You have a nerve coming here, Hunter, after what Mr Corday has told me.'

'Well I shouldn't take it too much to heart. Ain't but a little bit of old Garth's pride hurt. Now the professor, he got a bullet in the leg and the livery man's lost a horse ...'

'Why are you here?' McMurdo asked bluntly.

'I'd've thought you'da figured that out by now. I'm looking for my brother, Tom Hunter. Paid you a visit a few days back. Said he was going out to your mine and he never came back.' Chad remained by the door as he spoke, right hand hanging close to the butt of his Colt Frontier, the thumb of his left hand hooked into his gunbelt. There was an exchange of glances between the two that told Chad a whole lot more than words could have done.

'Yes, he did pay us a visit,' McMurdo agreed and

smiled, his earlier hostility forgotten. 'A most agreeable young man as I recall.' He frowned. 'You say he never reurned to his hotel? Most odd. He said nothing about going elsewhere when he left us.' With elbows on the arms of his chair, McMurdo steepled his hands before his face, peering across at Chad before saying heavily, 'I'm sorry to say, Mr Hunter, that it is not uncommon for folks travelling alone in this area to disappear. Indians.' He shook his head and his jowls wobbled. 'We have an Indian problem here. Bunch of renegade Navahos resent our mining activity on their sacred mountain. There have been quite a few attacks on parties travelling in the area of Squaw Mountain, over the past few months. The army keep promising to send a troop of men out and an Indian Agent is supposed to be coming to try and talk the problem out with them.' He shrugged. 'Until such times as either happens, the problem remains. Isn't that so, Mr Corday?'

'It's rough country out here,' Corday responded. 'Things can happen to a lone rider.'

'Which, I fear, may have happened to your brother,' McMurdo hurried on rapidly. 'Under the circumstances I'm sure we can persuade Mr Corday to forget the unfortunate incident in Prosperity. After all he has his horse back, the rifles have been returned and as you so rightly pointed out, only pride has been hurt here.'

Chad could only stare and wonder at the gall of the man. He was turning everything around to make it appear as though the professor, Cora and he were the aggressors.

'I'll tell that to the bullet hole in the professor's leg,' Chad shot back sarcastically.

'A regrettable accident,' McMurdo sighed. 'Unfortunately when Mr Corday went to offer his help the young lady, rather excitable type I shouldn't wonder, mistook his intentions and almost killed him. I take full blame for ordering those good people off company land in the first place. You see there had been pilfering at the mine and that reflects back on me. The professor and his daughter could have been accomplices of the thieves, the gold being passed to them. Unfortunately I acted all too hastily.' He shrugged and pulled a sorrowful face. 'What can I say? But I'm sure amends can be made and this whole lamentable series of accidents and errors forgotten.'

Chad eyed him in admiration. It was beautifully put and not a tone of false sincerity out of place. It was, of course, a lie from start to finish, but beautifully done.

'I swear, McMurdo, you could talk a thirsty man into believing he's drunk a barrel of water.'

'I'm sorry,' McMurdo looked genuinely puzzled. 'I don't understand what you are saying, Mr Hunter.'

Chad almost applauded that.

'Forget it, McMurdo, but just for my peace of mind, what part did the dead fella at the professor's camp have in all this?'

'No part, Mr Hunter. He was the victim of a cave-in at the mine. He was trapped for several hours. Unfortunately his mind snapped. He ran off when we got him free. He died at the Wellbeloveds' camp. Apparently he suffered internal injuries that led to his death. A most unfortunate and distressing incident. He was well liked and will be greatly missed – but about your brother. I can organize a search party, but I fear that after all this time, I doubt he will be found.'

'Don't trouble yourself,' Chad said. 'I'll find out for myself.'

'No trouble, Mr Hunter, your brother was most complimentary about the conditions at the mine. It's the least I can do.'

'You're all heart, McMurdo. No doubt we'll be meeting again.' With that Chad left the office and returned to the boarding-house.

McMurdo glowered at the door after Chad's departure.

'That man means trouble,' he stated.

'Indios wants him,' Corday replied and McMurdo's eyes drifted to his.

'Then let the 'breed have him,' came the curt reply.

'The man has the nerve of the devil,' the professor said after Chad had relayed the outcome of the meeting with McMurdo.

'Devil or not, I'm as hungry as a horse. You folks eating?' Chad said.

The Secret of Squaw Mountain

'Pa?' Cora looked at her father.

'You go on with Chad, dear. I'll get something sent up. I have some notes to go through and then I think I'll get an early night.'

Chad and Cora dined at a small restaurant across from the boarding-house. It was a pleasant experience for Chad who was more used to hash-houses and a novel one in being with a woman like Cora. Chad's dalliances with the opposite sex were usually of the saloon type. Unfortunately the edge was taken from his enjoyment over concern about his brother. Later, when the meal was over, Chad walked Cora back to the boarding-house then took himself off to one of the two saloons Grand Mesa boasted.

Grand Mesa was a town that mixed cattlemen and miners. It was normally an explosive mix, but here it seemed to work well. Maybe it was due to the two saloons. The 'Trailhand' favoured the cattlemen while the rather grandly named 'Diggers Palace' the miners. Chad chose the latter. He was after information and people talked after a few beers. To further increase his chances he cast his eyes over the groups of card tables and selected one with three old-timers playing stud in one corner and carried a bottle of whiskey across.

'Mind if'n I join you gents for a hand or two?' he said as he wandered up to a vacant chair.

'Ain't no big stakes here, son. We play to pass the time and jaw a little.'

'Suits me,' Chad replied and sat himself down

facing the man who had spoken. He was a short, chunky individual whose remaining hair had slid down to his chin in an explosion of white. 'Figured you gents could stand a little whiskey, on me, 'stead o' that hoss piss you've been drinking.' He nodded at their beer mugs.

'Mighty generous of you, son. I ain't one to turn hospitality away. This 'ere's Deke.' Chad nodded to a rake-thin, gaunt-faced man to the old man's left. 'Pete.' Pete was a cheerful-looking, round-faced man. They all looked to be in their sixies. A good age for getting the jaw muscles going, Chad reflected.

'Ain't seen you around town afore, stranger. They call me Tumbleweed on account of the whiskers.'

'Chad,' Chad replied with a laugh. 'New in town.'

'Ain't you the one that fazed Corday?' It was Deke that spoke.

'Word gets around,' Chad commented. 'Had a little run-in with a gent of that name. Friend o' yours?'

'Seen better friends laying in the dust after a dog's passed by,' Deke replied. 'He's bad news that one.' Deke nodded his mournful face before pouring a generous measure of whiskey into his beer.

'You two gonna play or jaw?' Tumbleweed asked as he dealt the cards.

The night wore on and time passed pleasantly

for Chad as he gently, unhurriedly, probed for information.

'We all had reg'lar jobs at the mine until McMurdo took over as manager,' Pete said at one time. 'Then he brought in his own men and had a stockade put up around the mine entrance, with lookout towers and all. Then if'n that weren't enough he strung up a barbed wire fence and employed Corday and his bully boys to police the area.' Pete scowled at his cards.

'Seems a lot of security,' Chad remarked.

'Man, a horsefly'll need a pass to get in there.'

Later, after Chad had taken a leak, he broached the subject of Indians.

'Heard tell of Injun raids,' Tumbleweed agreed. 'Squaw Mountain's sacred to 'em, Navahos that is. Utes couldn't give a cuss.'

'Used to be a tribe of Utes twenty miles west of the Squaw. They moved on soon after McMurdo took over,' Deke piped up. 'They was allus thieving.'

'What about the Williams family?' Pete said and Tumbleweed nodded. 'House burnt down, whole family gone. You 'member, Tumbleweed?'

'Should do. I was the first to happen on the burnt-out house, only …' He pulled a face at his cards and tossed the hand in with a sigh. 'Darned cards,' he moaned.

'Only what, Tumbleweed?' Chad prompted.

'They said it was Injuns and there was plenty of Injun sign about, fifteen, twenty horses, but the horses was shod. Ain't no Injuns ride shod horses.'

'Less'n they stoled 'em,' Deke said.

'Bullshit,' Tumbleweed scoffed.

'So what are you saying, Tumbleweed?' Chad asked.

'Don't rightly know, son. You figure it out.'

Chad folded in his hand and sat back. He was already doing that and didn't like the answer he was getting.

'There are some pretty weird stories concerning the Squaw,' Deke said. 'You in, Pete?'

'I'm in. You ain't getting my money without a fight, you old coot,' Pete replied.

'Hell, there's every type of story 'bout the Squaw. From a city of gold above the snowline, secret gold mines, demons and ghosts,' Tumbleweed jeered.

'More'n one man's vanished under mysterious circumstances on that old gel,' Deke said.

'In your head maybe,' Tumbleweed replied.

'Mind the time old Lobo Johnson went up on the Squaw looking for gold. Twenty years ago if'n it was a day. When he came offa her he was crazed out of his mind.'

'Lobo Johnson was mad 'afore he went up there,' Tumbleweed opined with a gap-toothed grin.

'Seen something that no mortal man was meant to see,' Deke continued, unabashed. 'See you.' He challenged Pete and clucked with delight as he covered Pete's two pairs with three eights and scooped in the pot. 'Old Navaho I once knew,' he lowered his voice causing the other three to lean forward to catch his words, 'He told me about a demon that's supposed to live up there above the treeline. Its name's "He-with-no-Voice", now ain't that some sorta name?' Deke gathered in the cards as a busty, blonde woman, face heavy wih make-up, overweight breasts straining the bodice of a tight, red dress, came up and draped a fleshy arm about Tumbleweed's shoulders. A stogie lanced from between her fingers.

'Hey, Tumbleweed, you got enough left to go a coupla rounds with old Suzie here?' she rasped from a smoke wrecked throat.

'Hell, Suzie, the mind's sure willing, but there ain't much of the old fire left below.'

'I'm sure we can raise a little spark, honey,' Suzie coaxed.

'Sure would be a little one too,' Tumbleweed brayed and Suzie withdrew, laughing.

Chad was laughing too as he pulled a timepiece from his pocket and found to his amazement it was almost midnight. The saloon was still full, although some customers were beginning to drift away, the air thick with smoke that hung in layers about the cobwebs of the ceiling and drifted about the hanging lamps.

'You in, Chad?' Deke asked, preparing to deal.

'One more and then I hit the sack.'

Chad's head was down as he eyed his cards, discarded two and watched idly as Deke dealt out two more.

'Hey, amigo, it's dying time.'

Chad's head snapped up. Indios stood some fifteen feet away behind Tumbleweed. The eyes in the gunman's dark-skinned face were flat and dead, without emotion. The silence that had followed his words became broken as chairs scraped and boots pounded as tables close by were hurriedly vacated. Chad's companions with them. Chad felt his heart rate increase a notch as he rose from his seat and stepped away from the table.

'Always is for somebody,' Chad replied evenly, showing no outward sign of the inner turmoil that churned. The silence in the saloon was almost deafening, filling his ears with a faint hiss.

'I said we would meet again,' Indios reminded him.

'There's no need for this,' Chad called.

'Wrong, amigo. Within me there is a great need,' Indios hissed. He flexed his black-gloved fingers and the joints crackled faintly.

The matched Colts appeared in his hands as if by magic. Such was the legendary speed of the man that all eyes were upon him, so that people could brag that they had seen his lightning double draw. The single shot that followed destroyed the ear-singing silence with its bark. A red dot appeared dead centre of the gunman's forehead, an insignificant speck. The hole that appeared at the back of the man's head was something totally different. As large as a fist, it sprayed blood, bone, brain and hair in a gory stream.

The bullet threw Indios back and slammed him to the floor without him even firing a shot. People stared in blank, almost supernatural, disbelief at Indios's intended victim as Chad eased the hammer back and returned the Colt Frontier to its holster.

'Jesus, son. If'n I hadn't seen it with my own eye ...' Tumbleweed took a step forward, hands shaking from the tension of the moment.

Slowly Chad released his pent-up breath as the saloon came alive with sound once again. He stepped back to the table and picked up the two cards Deke had dealt him earlier. With a wry smile mingling with the strain still on his face, he tossed the hand into the middle of the table.

'Guess it's not my lucky day,' he said and without another word or glance at the dead gunman, headed for the batwings and the cool night beyond.

FIVE

The tension had drained from Chad as he quietly mounted the stairs of the boarding-house to his room. It had been a long time since he had played out a fast-gun draw and the adrenalin still surged, making him feel slightly light-headed. He entered his room and struck a match to the lamp on the cupboard by the window that looked out over a dark backlot. He kept the light low as he removed his coat and gunbelt.

'I was wondering when you'd be back,' a voice called softly from the bed behind. He spun around, shocked.

Cora smiled shyly at him from the shadows of the bed. She was half lying, half sitting against the pillows, one hand holding the sheets to her neck. He could see that her shoulders were bare.

'Cora. What the ...?' His voice was a rasping whisper as he took a step towards the bed, the lamp throwing his shadow across it.

Cora wriggled upright, the springs of the bed creaking softly. She let the sheet slide from her breasts as she eyed him.

Chad felt a hot glow rush through him.

'Come to bed, Chad,' Cora invited huskily.

Chad took another faltering step.

'Cora, I ...' He was suddenly aware that he didn't know what to say, his eyes spoke for him as they drifted from the hard-nippled breasts to the sweet face above, haloed in the long, chestnut hair.

With a giggle, Cora threw back the sheets and, naked, came towards him. Her perfume filled his nostrils as she laced her hands behind his neck and pulled his face down onto hers, lips meshing together. His fingers ran over her velvet-soft flesh and desire grew hungrily within him. She broke away and began to undo the buttons of his shirt. Chad was unable to stop himself. He wanted her as much as she wanted him. Before climbing into bed he doused the lamp.

McMurdo listened with open-mouthed disbelief to the story Corday shakily told, after Corday's pounding at the hotel door, where he had a permanent room, roused the mine manager from a deep sleep.

'I thought you said the 'breed was the best,' McMurdo complained.

'He was until Hunter came along,' Corday protested.

'Then you'd better find someone faster or take him on yourself,' McMurdo snarled. 'That's your job, that's what you get paid for. But remember, Corday. Things are sweet for us here. Don't louse it up. Now get out of here and let me get some sleep.'

McMurdo was still awake as the first grey light of day spread out from the eastern horizon, his mind grappling with the problems that Chad Hunter and the Wellbeloveds presented. The latter he could dispose of relatively easily, it was Hunter that presented the real problem. He would have to be got rid of before he could put his plan for the professor and his daughter into operation.

Chad opened his eyes to find the bedroom filled with muted light from the curtained window. Cora was gone. He had not heard her leave. He climbed groggily from the bed and dappled his face with cold water from a jug by the washstand. It helped to wake him up. Later, shaved and dressed, he went downstairs to find the small dining-room full as boarders breakfasted. The buzz of conversation stopped as Chad entered, appreciating the aroma of bacon that hung heavy and appetizingly in the air. He nodded at the silent people who watched his progress across the room to the corner table occupied by the professor and Cora.

' 'Morning, Chad,' Cora greeted. There was a sparkle in her eye.

'Cora. Professor.'

The Secret of Squaw Mountain 61

'Sit down, m'boy. Coffee?'

'Please, Professor. How's the leg?'

'Much better, thanks. Now what have you got to say for yourself after last night?'

Chad looked up guiltily, mouth dropping open. Cora spluttered over a mouthful of coffee and had to grab a napkin to press it to her mouth to mute a coughing fit that reddened her face.

'Sorry, Professor?' Chad said faintly.

'It might be early in the morning, but your clash with that Indios character in the saloon last night is all over town.'

Chad breathed a sigh of relief.

'I thought folks went a bit quiet when I came in,' he said softly, casting a quick glance around, but the guests had returned to their food and conversation was buzzing. 'Indios made his play and lost,' Chad said indifferently.

'What happened? What have I missed?' Cora asked.

'Chad here was forced into a gunfight with Corday's gunman, Indios, last night.'

'What happened?' Cora's eyes were wide as they flickered from man to man.

'Indios came second,' Chad replied as a tray of bacon and eggs was brought over for them to help themselves from.

'You never told me ...' Cora cut the sentence off with a guilty glance at her father who was in the process of helping himself from the tray.

'You wouldn't have known, dear. It was long

after you were in bed.' He eyed Chad. 'You seem to have become a local hero.'

'It'll blow over,' Chad said dismissively, hoping that it would, but knowing that he'd be the target for any aspiring gunsel hoping to pick up a reputation.

Over breakfast Chad told them what he had learned from the three old-timers.

'So it would seem that McMurdo is running a slave labour force,' the professor mused. 'The question is why? What is he getting out of it?'

'I haven't figured that out yet.' Chad drained his second cup of coffee. They were the only ones left at breakfast now. 'I reckon Tom found out and they're holding him at the mine.' He did not wish to dwell on the alternative until he had no other option.

'What do you intend to do now?' the professor asked.

'Take a ride out to the mine and have a look around.'

'You will be careful, Chad?' Cora put in quickly.

'Careful is my middle name from now on,' Chad replied with a grin.

Later Cora walked with him to the livery and as he saddled his mare in the warm, hay- and horse droppings-smelling barn, said reproachfully, 'You might have told me about the fight.'

He straightened from tightening the cinch and faced her. 'As I recall I didn't get much of a chance to say anything.'

She coloured at his words and then smiled coyly. 'I guess not.' She reached up and kissed him on the cheek. 'Please take care, Chad,' she repeated her earlier plea.

'I'll be back,' he promised, little knowing that the promise was going to be a mite harder to keep than he imagined.

On the way out of town he was waved down by Roy Cooper, the sheriff, his moustached face bleak.

'I'd appreciate you leaving town as soon as possible.' His words were blunt.

'Now hold on, Sheriff. It was a fair fight. Indios did the prodding. Ask anyone who was there.'

'If'n it hadn't been you'd be in jail now,' Cooper pointed out. 'You've picked up a reputation, mister, that's gonna bring half the gunsels in the territory into Grand Mesa looking to try you out. I don't need that kinda trouble.' Cooper reaffirmed what Chad already knew.

'I'll go when I'm ready, Sheriff, and that'll be as soon as I've found out what's happened to my brother,' Chad replied quietly, hazel eyes hardening until Cooper began to squirm uneasily beneath his unsmiling gaze.

A weasel-faced man watched as Chad rode slowly from the town and headed towards Squaw Mountain, then he hurried to the EM Mining office.

Chad hunkered down amid the rocks and stared

with wonder at the mine. Heat rose from the rocks and the sun lay hot on his back. The structure he looked at did indeed resemble a stockade. On three sides the rough, timber walls rose twenty feet into the air. The fourth was the rock face itself and the mine entrance. The two outer corners contained square lookout towers, with a third one the width of the entrance gates it overlooked. Dark smoke from a smelting bed rose lazily above the stockade.

It was set at the end of a blind canyon, one of many that fissured the ground at the base of Squaw Mountain. To the rear and left of the stockade the canyon wall rose sheer to a hundred feet or more, but where he now lay was a low ridge of rock, the remains of a wall between two canyons. It was a ridge that did not give him enough height to look down into the compound of the stockade. A few stumpy, twisted scrub oak grew amid the rocks and mingled with thorny brush to afford him some cover from the men in the towers. He had tethered his mare in a small arroyo out of sight of the stockade.

The mouth of the canyon, narrower than the wide body, was strung with a high, barbed wire fence with yet more armed guards stationed within. Chad had never seen such high security on a mine before. He viewed the scene before him with growing dismay. The area before the stockade offered no cover to approach it unseen and even if he did he still had the problem of the twenty-foot, guarded walls to get over. Maybe darkness was the best time?

Stones clattered behind him. He rolled over, dragging the Colt Frontier from its holster, only to see the stock of a rifle swinging towards him. He caught a brief glimpse through squinting eyes of Corday's grinning face, then the hardwood stock thudded hard over his right ear and his world went black.

The light coming through the door grille painted a distorted picture of the barred opening on the opposite wall. Chad groaned as he sat up, the movement setting hammers beating rhythmically in his head. He dragged himself across the rough, uneven floor and sat with his back to the wall next to the door. The rough wall bit coldly into his back. It was only after the hammering subsided to a bearable level that he realized he was without hat, coat or shirt. Along with these missing items went his gunbelt, boots and socks.

From his position he took stock of his surroundings. The room was no more than ten feet square and eight feet high, carved from the living rock. Apart from the shaft of dull, yellow light coming from beyond the door, there was no other source of illumination, leaving most of his prison cell, as he now called it, in darkness and shadow. He reached up, wincing as his fingers found the painful lump over his right ear and remembered Corday's grinning face above the clubbing rifle.

Slowly, painfully he climbed to his feet and staggered to the wooden door, gripping the metal bars in the foot-square opening and peering out into a narrow, stone-walled corridor. Straight ahead lay a door similar to his. To the left of that a kerosene lamp sat in a niche in the wall. He listened, from somewhere off to the right he heard a groaning.

'Hey, anybody out there?' he shouted, rattling the bars. The door shook a little in its frame. 'Is anybody there? Room service?' His voice fled up and down the dismal, stone corridor, breached by other doors.

'Who are you?' An unseen, answering voice came from his right.

'Hunter, Chad Hunter. Where are we?'

There was a dry, mirthless chuckle.

'In hell, mister. That's where we's at,' came the sardonic reply.

Boots echoed from the left and a coarse voice yelled, 'Shut the talking, tunnel rats.'

A shadow fell across the grille. Two men, one big and burly, appeared at Chad's door. Small, mean eyes peered out at Chad from a fleshy, stubble darkened face.

'What's all the yelling fer, mister? Gonna wake the rest of the guests with that hollerin'.'

The second man, short and skinny, was the weasel-faced man who had watched Chad ride from Grand Mesa.

'That's telling him, Bull,' Weasel-face giggled,

showing large, crooked, yellow teeth.

'Step back from the door, mister,' Bull ordered, pulling a ring of keys from his belt. "Body wants a word with you.' Chad stepped back. A key rattled in the lock and seconds later the door swung open with a dry creak. 'Step out, mister. Won't do to keep the boss waiting.'

'Step on out, mister,' Weasel-face repeated and giggled. Both were darkly clad in a sombre mixture of brown and black and each toted a gunbelt. In addition Bull carried a Winchester.

'Real nice of you folks,' Chad smiled cordially as he emerged. 'Does your monkey do tricks?' he nodded at Weasel-face and the man's face dropped to a sullen, angry expression.

'Guess you'll have to learn the hard way, mister,' Bull sighed mysteriously. 'Move!' He indicated to the left with the barrel of the Winchester.

As Chad turned his back Weasel-face darted forward, an eight-inch, leather cosh gripped in one hand. Chad detected sudden movement at his back, but before he could turn, pain exploded through his insides as the cosh slammed the area above his kidneys. The blows brought a cry of pain to his lips and he fell to his knees, face creased in agony, body gripped in paralyzing pain.

'Shouldn't be talking about ol' Polecat that way, mister.' Bull's voice sounded close to his left ear. 'He might be small, but he knows a hundred ways to cause a man pain. I'd advise you to get up afore he gets mad at you.'

With an effort Chad climbed stiffly to his feet, turned and stared with pain-filled eyes at the two, Polecat in particular.

'I'll remember that.' He looked into Polecat's eyes. 'You can bet on that.'

'Quit jawing, mister and move out,' Bull prompted.

Chad was herded down the corridor to the left. Light showed ahead and on rounding a bend he found his way barred by a pair of iron gates that opened into the compound behind the stockade. As Bull hollered to a man outside to unlock the gates, Chad reflected dully that he had found a way into the stockade, but not quite as he expected.

The hidden sun flowed across the west wall and clipped the upper edge of the east wall with a band of red. The lookout towers were bathed in the orangy-red glow while the compound itself was filled with a purple half-light. Chad realized with a jolt that it was getting close to nightfall. He had been unconscious for several hours.

He was taken across the compound littered with rock heaps towards a low, cabin structure set against the east wall. Under the west wall lay a long bunkhouse. The entrance to the mine was a gaping, fifteen feet square hole that led into darkness. From it came a narrow gauge track that entered the long, low smelting shed at one end, emerged at the other and returned to the mine.

The sharp fragments of rock that littered the

The Secret of Squaw Mountain

ground dug cruelly into the soles of Chad's feet and he was limping by the time he was ushered into the cabin. Behind a desk, smoking a cigar, sat the fat McMurdo. Garth Corday, smiling as usual, leaned against the wall by the window from which he had watched Chad being brought in.

'We meet again, Mr Hunter, as you so rightly pointed out at our last meeting.' He sounded jovial and amiable.

'Don't think much of the accommodation here,' Chad remarked lightly.

'Wait outside you two,' McMurdo directed at Bull and Polecat and eyed Chad through a haze of smoke. 'You are a predictable man, Mr Hunter, and predictable men are easy to catch. I knew you'd head for the mine and had Polecat watching for you. As soon as you left town he came and told me and after that it was simple.' He shook his head in mock disappointment. 'I thought better things of you.'

'Sorry I didn't come up to expectations. Perhaps next time?'

'Don't fool yourself, Mr Hunter, there will be no next time. Your disappearance will not be mourned by the good people of Grand Mesa. You will become another victim of an Indian raid. I don't mind telling you now that you had me worried at the time, but as it turned out that was a needless worry. All that remains are the Wellbeloveds and once they are out of the way I shan't need to worry again.'

'They are no threat to you, McMurdo. Leave them alone,' Chad warned.

'Oh, I will not touch them, though I doubt the Navahos on Squaw Mountain will be so generous of nature.'

'What do you mean?' Chad took a step forward, fists balling at his sides.

'The professor was made an offer he could not refuse. He and his daughter are somewhere on Squaw Mountain at this very moment, preparing to camp for the night. Alas, it will be their last night. By noon tomorrow they will become genuine victims of the Indians.' McMurdo laughed. With a murderous rage boiling through him, Chad threw himself forward, trying to get at the man. Corday, anticipating such a move, stepped in and the barrel of his gun cracked across Chad's temple, splitting the skin and sending Chad to his knees. It was a position Chad was finding himself in more and more lately.

'Very gallant, Mr Hunter, but I'm afraid it's time you were put to work.' He called Bull and Polecat in and as they hoisted Chad to his feet, continued, 'We shall not be meeting again. Good-bye, Hunter.'

It was no coincidence that earlier that very day Beau Trasker and the professor should meet. It was not a meeting that had been made in heaven, as the professor first thought, but in McMurdo's office.

When Cora returned from seeing Chad off she found her father in the small parlour of the boarding-house, deep in conversation with a tall, handsome cowboy. Both looked up as she entered.

'Come, dear. See what Mr Trasker has brought us.' The professor was in a high state of excitement. His eyes positively glowed with delight. She was uncomfortably aware of the stranger's appraising gaze as she crossed the room to her father's side. 'See!' He held out a small, brown, earthenware bowl. 'It's a genuine Anasazi bowl.'

Cora took the bowl gingerly, turning it in her hands before handing it back to her father.

'It's real, Pa?'

'Very much so.' The professor's head bobbed up and down. 'And Mr Trasker knows where more can be found.' He beamed his pleasure.

'Beau, ma'am. Beau Trasker at your service.' He swept his hat off to reveal a mass of blond, curly hair set atop his lean, handsome face. He smiled and fixed her with a blue-eyed stare. 'Sure is a pleasure meeting you, Miss Cora, if'n I can be so bold? Your pappy here's been telling me all about you.' His slow, Texas drawl settled pleasingly on the ear. He was clad in a frilled, tan, buckskin jacket over a blue, calico shirt with dusty blue levis and scuffed black leather boots. There was a natural friendliness about him that put her at her ease and swept away any earlier misgivings.

'Just plain Cora will do, Mr Trasker,' she replied with a smile.

'They for sure can't call you plain, Cora,' Beau returned gallantly and she felt her cheeks redden. In order to cover her embarrassment she said quickly,

'Where did you get the bowl, Mr Trasker?'

'Beau please, Cora,' he said as she settled in a high-backed chair next to her father. He remained standing. 'Why, up on the old Squaw.'

'Tell her what else you saw, Mr Trasker,' the professor prompted excitedly.

'Sure thing, sir. Like I was telling your pappy. There I was, just pokin around in this lil' ol' canyon when I came upon a whole passel of buildings built into the canyon wall. I tell you now, Cora, I ain't seen the likes of it afore. Well, it was in one of the buildings that I came across the little fella your pappy's holding and there are a whole load more of 'em.'

'You see, I was right.' The professor was bubbling over with joy. 'The Anasazi did reach this far and built one of their canyon cities on Squaw Mountain.'

'Ain't run across those boys afore,' Beau said with a frown.

'That's not surprising, Mr Trasker. They died out some five hundred years ago,' the professor said.

'Is that a fact? Ain't that purely somethin',"
Beau breathed.

'What about the Indians that are up there? We were told they were dangerous,' Cora said.

The Secret of Squaw Mountain

'Grey Wolf and his Navahos?' Beau looked surprised. 'Heck, Cora, they ain't after no trouble. Kinda friendly bunch of folks.'

'As I've said all along. Gossip and old wives' tales,' the professor jeered.

'Surely is,' Beau agreed. 'Why them Navahos are as peaceful as a spring day. Ain't out for making mischief, 'cepting in white folks' minds.'

'Mr Trasker is willing to take us to the Anasazi city,' the professor cried.

'Be my pure pleasure,' Beau threw in.

'But, dad, what about your leg?' Cora protested.

'My leg is all right,' came the snapped back answer.

'We should wait for Chad.'

'Chad has his own problems, Cora. Looking for his brother takes precedence over Anasazi ruins. He may not come back for days and even then not be inclined to come with us. With Mr Trasker as our guide we can be at the Anasazi city by nightfall tomorrow if we leave straight away.'

'Leave now?' She looked dismayed at the thought. It was all too sudden. 'But we need a wagon, supplies ...'

'Can't get a wagon up a mountain, ma'am,' Beau pointed out. 'Just need a horse apiece and a coupla packmules to carry supplies. Take no time at all to organize. I can do that while you folks pack whatever you need.'

'But ...' Cora began.

'No buts, Cora,' the professor said angrily. 'We

have almost reached our objective after months of searching. I for one am not going to pass up the opportunity now that it is in our grasp.'

They had set out at noon and now, as the sun reddened in the western sky, filling cracks and fissures with purple shadow, they were high on Squaw Mountain with night falling.

There had been no sign of the Navahos and Beau rode, talking amiably, without a care in the world. His open, unworried manner helped dispel her fears. She knew her father had been right about Chad, but even so his presence would have been an added comfort. She had left a note at the boarding-house for him and, as she busied herself gathering dry scrub for a fire, she wondered what he was doing now.

SIX

If there was a hell-on-earth it was here, deep in the complex of tunnels that made up the Squaw Mountain gold mine. Chad was taken to the workface at the end of a long tunnel. Here he joined twenty others who hacked at the rock face, digging out the veins of gold ore that striated the rock face with bands of yellow. Kerosene lamps dotted about niches in the walls provided an inadequate light that cast moving shadows over the walls as workers moved to and fro.

Chad was shocked at what he saw. There were men and women there working side by side. Their feet were bare and like him their backs were shirtless. This applied to two of the women workers, the others managing to maintain their dignity with the tattered remnants of their upper clothing. The bodies of both men and women were criss-crossed with nasty weals from the whips the brutish guards carried and Chad felt anger seethe within him.

Polecat had used his cosh enthusiastically on

the small of Chad's back as they reached the working area, sending Chad to his knees again. He was prompted to his feet as the leather thong of a whip lashed across his shoulders, leaving a red welt smarting in its wake.

Chad joined a man who was loading chunks of gold ore into a rickety wheelbarrow. He found out later that the ore was wheeled to a waiting ore-truck in a large cave at the far end of the tunnel. The man was thin and gaunt, hair wild and untidy about his head and cheeks and matted with dust.

'Another soul for hell,' the man uttered. 'You the one hollering earlier?'

'Chad Hunter,' Chad replied. It was hot in the mine and sweat was beginning to break over Chad's body as he worked, loading the wheelbarrow.

'Had me a name once,' the man mused as he humped a chunk of ore into the creaking barrow. There were four other barrows there. 'Yates, I think.'

'How long have you been here?' Chad asked.

'For ever,' came the reply.

They worked in silence for a while, the only sound coming from the metal picks striking at the yellow-veined wall and the spiteful crack of the whip accompanied by a gruff curse from a guard.

'If'n you're lucky you might get ore-cart detail,' the man spoke again. A wistful smile chased across his face. 'You take it to the surface an' see the sky. Man, that sure is something, to see the sky.' As he finished speaking a tear crept from the man's right eye and tracked a path down his lined, dirty face. He wiped it away quickly and busied himself loading the barrow. Chad experienced shock and pity and then fury. A burning rage at what one human being was inflicting on others.

'Has anyone ever escaped from here?'

Chad's question brought a smile to the thin face.

'Sure, quite a few.'

'How?' Chad demanded.

'They died.' A cackle fell from his dirt-encrusted lips. 'Death is the only way out of here, mister.' He was quiet for a few more moments. 'Hunter, you say? Seems to me I recognize that name from somewhere.'

Chad stopped what he was doing and grabbed he man's wrist.

'Tom Hunter, my brother. You've seen him?'

'Hell, mister, I don't know.' Yates broke the grip, eyes frightened. 'Just heard the name that's all.'

Chad would have pursued the matter further but a whip cracked across his back. He spun as fire flared through his shoulders, to face a stocky, grinning guard.

'Talking ain't allowed, rat turd. Get working or get more of this.' He held up the whip in his right hand while his left hand rested on the butt of an

Army Colt. Chad's eyes flashed and for an insant his body tensed as though he was going to leap at his aggressor, but common sense prevailed. He said nothing and turned back to his work.

It was hard, tedious work. The sharp rock cut into his hands and fragments on the ground bit into his feet. Chad tried to forget his own discomfort by studying his companions. Some were Indians, but most were white. No one spoke and their eyes in the dusty, yellow gloom were dull and lifeless. The ten guards moved back and forth, encouraging greater activity with vicious use of the whips they carried.

Chad had no idea of the time, but his muscles felt as though they hadn't stopped for a week. He had just returned from loading the ore into one of the metal ore-carts when a man, thin to the point of starvation, collapsed at the rock face. Chad dropped the barrow and went forward, reaching the man and turning him over gently. The man's face was grey, his breathing laboured. With a shock Chad realized that the thin, lined face belonged to a man younger than he. The man's bony body was torn and scarred, ridged with lines of scar tissue. The man tried to speak, but no words came from his dry throat.

'This man needs help!' Chad shouted. The next second the handle of a whip was used to club the side of his head and rough hands dragged him from the stricken man and threw him to one side. All work had stopped. The one who had clubbed

Chad was the stocky man from earlier.

'Get up, rat turd,' he growled at the man, stirring him with the toe of his boot. The man tried to rise, but the effort was too much. He fell back into a sitting position against the rock face.

A whip lashed out, the tip opening a six-inch gash across the man's chest. Though it caused pain the man was too far gone to help himself. The guard wielding the whip grinned. A half dozen more lashes and blood flowed down the victim's chest. Coiling the whip the guard calmly took out his gun and shot the man through the head. The sound of the shot was deafening in the close confines of the tunnel and had the other workers whimpering and covering their ears.

'Get back to work, all of you,' the man barked and the other guards moved in, using whips and feet. Two of them stepped in and, gripping the dead man by an ankle apiece, dragged him away, leaving an ominous red trail in the dirt of the floor.

'Another one for the abyss,' Chad's companion muttered. 'See, mister, that's the only way out, with a bullet for company.'

The savage, inhuman treatment meted out to the slave workers filled Chad with a murderous rage that he found hard to contain. Innocent travellers, searching for a new life, full of hopes and dreams that were cruelly shattered by McMurdo's capture and imprisonment of them. Chad had known tight spots before in his life, but none as deadly as this. Somehow he would have to escape and soon, before his will was ground down and he became like the others. Wrapped up in his thoughts he had not noticed the arrival of Bull and Polecat with another slave who carried a bucket of brackish water.

'Water up!' Bull bellowed and Chad looked up as work came to a halt all around him and the slaves lined up on either side, facing inward. Yates gestured to him and Chad fell in beside him.

'Water call,' Yates whispered. 'Only chance yer git and sometimes not then if'n a guard thinks you ain't worked hard enough.'

Flanked by Bull and Polecat, the water carrier dished out a ladleful of water to each slave in turn. The stocky guard who had shot the slave earlier, followed up. Chad had found out that his name was Drayton.

Chad brushed sweat from his eyes as the group drew closer, aware of how dry his throat was. His eyes settled on the partially obscured slave with the water. Dirty and half naked, head bowed as he worked, never looking at the person receiving the water, as though by not seeing this hideous world did not exist. Chad's heart quickened and as his turn came and the man stood, head bowed before him, Chad said:

'Tom?'

The man's head jerked up. Dark, unkempt hair parted and his eyes fell on Chad, widening.

The Secret of Squaw Mountain

'Chad.' The name fell hoarsely from his throat. 'Chad, is it you?' The bucket fell from the man's hand, but dropped on its bottom and did not spill as Tom Hunter gripped his brother's shoulders, eyes still not believing.

'It's me, Tom.' Chad became aware of Bull and Polecat grinning broadly.

'Ain't it nice to bring kin together?' Bull sang out.

'One o' life's pure pleasures,' Polecat agreed and then lashed the side of Tom's head with his cosh. Tom cried out, holding his head and staggering sideways. He tripped over the bucket as he went down and the bucket tipped, sloshing its contents over the dusty floor. 'Pleasure time is over,' he ended with a snarl and eyed Chad. The man had not moved. 'Guess you're starting to learn,' Polecat said, grinning wolfishly.

'Maybe I am,' Chad agreed, still battling the urge to leap on the weasel-faced man. The time would come.

'Ain't that somethin',' Bull crooned. 'No water left. Pure shame for you folks.' The tone of his voice and grin on his face belied the words he spoke.

'Please, we must have water.' A woman detached herself from the line facing Chad.

Polecat stepped forward to intercept her.

'*Must* eh?' His small eyes ranged over the woman. Beneath the dirt and grime she was blonde and pretty. 'What's it worth for me to give you water, woman?' Polecat leered.

'Worth? I d ... don't understand,' she said in confusion.

'Sure you do,' Polecat coaxed and with one hand reached out and ripped open her tattered, cotton blouse. She staggered back using her arms to cover her nakedness. 'You know what ol' Polecat wants,' the weasel-faced man breathed and rubbed the front of his pants suggestively while the watching guards laughed and jeered.

Polecat stepped closer to the frightened woman who was backed against the wall hugging herself. He tried to prise her arms apart with the cosh, but when this did not work he used the cosh on her face, slapping it back and forth, forcing her to raise her arms in protection.

'That's better,' Polecat smiled as he took hold of one of her full breasts and began to knead and squeeze the flesh. Chad saw the woman close her eyes and submit to the man's unwelcome attentions while the guards offered coarse suggestions.

'Leave her alone, shit-head!' Chad could no longer stand to see a person, especially a woman, humiliated so.

Polecat stiffened and the jeering stopped. Heads turned in Chad's direction. Polecat turned away from the woman, eyes settling on Chad.

'Now that weren't a very neighbourly thing to say,' Polecat hissed.

'Told you afore, mister. Don't do to rile ol' Polecat. He got ways to make you hurt where you didn't think you could hurt,' Bull said.

The Secret of Squaw Mountain

Chad tensed himself. He thought he was ready for any move the weasel-faced man might make. Polecat suckered him by slowly drawing his gun. Suckered him enough to get his attention the same second he swung the cosh between Chad's legs.

Chad cried out in agony as pain flowed, like liquid fire, from his genitals into his gut. He doubled over, clutching himself, bile rising acrid and burning into his throat.

'Seems I was wrong, you ain't learned anything yet,' Polecat declared viciously. All eyes were now on Polecat and Chad. None saw the man standing closest to the rock face retrieve a pick and start forward, but they did hear his yell. It echoed through the gloom and shadows like some long-forgotten warrior-cry. A woman screamed.

'Amos!' It was the blonde woman.

Heads were turning as one curved, metal arm of the pick dug into Polecat's back. Bone snapped and cracked. Through tear-blurred eyes Chad saw the point of the pick emerge, red and dripping, from the centre of Polecat's chest.

Polecat gave a hoarse scream that broke down into a bubbling gurgle as blood exploded from his gaping mouth. He gripped the exposed tip of the pick, eyes wild and staring as he staggered this way and that, his shadow gyrating in a grotesque dance over the walls. Then he tipped forward and slammed face down on the floor.

There was a moment of shocked, disbelieving

silence, then pandemonium broke loose as Bull and the guards turned on the man called Amos who now stood in slack-armed silence, face expressionless. Ignoring his own pain, Chad saw the chance that he had been waiting for. The rest of the slaves were forgotten. He moved quietly behind a stunned guard, wrapped an arm about his throat and at the same time drew the man's Colt. The weapon spat flame in Chad's hand and three of the guards went down. One of them was Drayton. Bull clawed his weapon from its holster and fired back. The bullets thudded into the body of the man Chad was holding and he slumped in Chad's grip.

Confusion and fear reigned. Bullets began to fly in all directions. Chad saw Yates and another man fall. Releasing his hold of the dead man he dived behind one of the ore barrows. Bullets followed him, splintering the wooden sides and ricocheting from the ore rock. Chad loosed off two more shots, one finding its mark. He rolled onto his back as a shadow loomed. Bull, face crazed with hate, was pointing his gun at him. Chad pulled the trigger of his own weapon only to have the hammer fall on an empty chamber.

Bull's lips rolled back in a wide grin.

'You're dead, mister,' he rasped.

There was movement behind Bull. Chad caught a brief glimpse of the blonde-haired woman. A kerosene lamp smashed against the side of Bull's head, knocking his hat off and dousing him in spilled oil. He sidestepped drunkenly, the gun wavering away from Chad and the next instant his head became engulfed in a ball of flame. Bull screamed through the flames, dropped the gun and began clawing at his head. The flames popped and crackled as the flesh blistered and cracked and filled the air with the stench of burning hair and flesh. The remaining guards lost their nerve and ran down the tunnel along with the terrified slaves, away from the work face and death as Bull flailed about, hitting the wall and bouncing away, his terrible death cries becoming less, until finally he fell across an ore-filled barrow and became still, the crackling flames fading from the blistered, bubbling flesh.

Chad came to his feet, tossing the empty gun aside. He quickly went across to the dead guards and took their handguns. He shoved one into his brother's limp hand. The woman had moved next to the man now. Chad gave them both a gun.

'We haven't got much time, so let's make use of it. Come on!' He grabbed Tom's arm and propelled him down the tunnel to the central cave where the ore was loaded into the ore-carts. The woman and man followed. The cave was deserted, but once the initial panic was over the guards would be back and in force. There were four other exits. Chad discounted the one laid with tracks for the ore-carts. That would be the way McMurdo's men would come.

'Which way?' He turned on the three.

'You sure have a way of livening up the place,' Tom remarked shakily as he recovered from the shock of events that had seemed to have taken a lifetime, yet had taken, at the most, five minutes.

'Let's hope we can hold onto our lives long enough to keep it lively,' Chad replied grimly. 'Now which way?' As he searched their faces for an answer, it was supplied by distant shouts and many booted feet coming from the tunnel the metal tracks disappeared into. Chad indicated the opening ahead. 'That way.' He ushered them forward into the opening. It was not a moment too soon. A hail of bullets followed them in, hitting rock and screaming away into the darkness beyond the lamplit gloom that bathed the entrance. They hunkered down in the darkness, facing the entrance that showed as a bright, ragged circle. Anyone rash enough to appear in it would make an easy target.

In the quiet minutes that followed Chad introduced himself and his brother to the man and woman and learned that they were Amos and Kate Bradley, husband and wife, Amos as fair-haired as his wife.

'I want to thank you, Amos, for doing what you did back there.'

'I should be thanking you for saving Kate,' Amos countered. 'And if'n it all ends here, neither of us could hope for better companions.'

'Let's hope it don't get that far,' Chad replied with a grin.

'Hey in there!' They all stiffened as Corday's voice floated back to them from the entrance. Chad could not see him. The man was keeping out of sight. 'You picked the wrong one, Hunter.' There was triumph in Corday's voice. 'The wrong one for you, that is. That tunnel ain't used but for one thing and that's the dead. The only place it leads to is the abyss and you won't like that.'

Corday's laugh echoed down the tunnel and filled their ears.

SEVEN

'I've heard mention of this abyss afore,' Chad said softly. 'What does it mean?'

A bitter smile crossed the face of Amos.

'It's where they put the dead, Chad. This place tends to use people up pretty quick. When someone dies their bodies are taken to the abyss and dropped in. I guess this tunnel leads to that place.'

'Very convenient,' Chad commented dryly.

'Hello in the tunnel?' Corday's voice floated in to them while he himself remained out of sight. 'Give yourself up now and you'll be treated fair.'

A smile spread across Chad's face.

'That's a mighty fine offer, Garth, but I gotta better one. Why don't you come in and get us?'

'Suit yourself, Hunter. There ain't but one way outta that hell-hole and me and the boys'll be waiting and the longer we wait the worse it'll be for you. Maybe them folks in there with you ain't of a mind to die along with you.'

Chad looked at the three in turn.

'You heard the man, take your choice. Stay here or go.'

It was Amos who gave the reply.

'Go to hell, Corday.'

'There's your answer, Garth. Best tell McMurdo he's got a riot on his hands.'

'Have it your way for now, Hunter. Without food or water you won't last long and we've got all the time in the world.' A laugh followed his words.

Chad looked around. The darkness at their backs was absolute. The only light lay back the way they had come in the shape of two lamps set either side of the tunnel.

'Cover me,' Chad said and, crossing to the far side of the tunnel, moved forward at a crouch, his own weapon ready. No one was foolish enough to stick their heads around the tunnel entrance. He retrieved one lamp and scurried back to them.

'What's the plan, Chad?' Tom asked.

'Best we find this abyss and take it from there.'

With Chad in the lead the group moved into the Stygian depths. After a few yards the tunnel curved to the right and the entrance became lost from sight.

'Looks to be the remains of an old working,' Tom said after a few moments. 'This place is a honeycomb of such tunnels.'

Deeper they went, wrapped in a cocoon of yellow light thrown by the lamp. Kate had managed to repair her blouse to save her blushes. As they progressed deeper into the tunnel the air became tainted with a smell that grew stronger the further they went. It reminded Chad of rotting meat and his stomach began to churn as unpleasant thoughts as to its origins filled his mind.

The abyss stopped them thirty feet from the end of the tunnel, dropping away into black, unplumbed depths.

'The end of the road,' Tom observed grimly, his voice echoing away into the death tainted darkness.

Chad squatted and lowered the lamp below the edge of the pit. It was from the blackness of the pit that the awful stench was rising.

Kate screamed, the frantic sound bouncing about the walls, and turned away sobbing, stumbling away from the edge of the abyss to lean with one hand splayed against the wall for support, the other arm pressed tightly across her stomach. The men managed to stay in position, but only just. Twenty feet below them lay a scene that even the worst nightmare could not contend with.

In the thinly spread glow of the lamp, eyeless sockets, black and ragged, stared back at them from fleshless, yellow skulls. Jaws gaped with vindictive smiles above gleaming ribcages, all tangled together on a bed of dark shadows. But it was the other bodies that set the mind to screaming. Recent bodies clothed in purple, maggot-writhing flesh. There were four of these in

The Secret of Squaw Mountain

various stages of decay and it was from these that the stench came. Accompanying the dead in that awful pit were hordes of rats, their eyes red in the glow as they paused in their feasting and looked up, whether in fear or anticipation Chad could not say.

They had found the abyss!

'Jesus Christ!' Tom was the first of the men to turn away and Amos quickly followed, leaving Chad squatting on the rim, his hunched shadow vague and ghostly on the roof above.

Chad's eyes roamed the charnel depths, ignoring the stench of death that arose around him. He supposed that the abyss had been a natural hollow in the rock that the tunnel had collapsed into. He tried to pierce the dark shadows that lined the walls where they met the ground, but they refused to give up their secrets. His nostrils flared. Within the nauseating smell lay a coolness, a freshness. The stench should have been heavier. Air was getting into the abyss from somewhere below and the only way to find out where it was coming from was to go down into the awful pit.

He returned to the group and told them what he suspected about fresh air coming into the abyss.

'The only way to find out for sure is to go down and take a look,' he concluded grimly.

There was a startled silence at his words.

'You mean we've all got to go down?' Kate's voice was a shocked whisper, eyes wide and horrified.

'Depends on what I find when I get down there.'

'How are you going to get down?' Tom asked.

'Walls are pretty rough. Plenty of hand and footholds. Should be an easy climb.'

'But the rats?' Kate asked and Chad smiled bleakly.

'They seem to be well fed. Don't reckon they'll be much interested in moving food,' he said macabrely.

'And what if they're not?' Tom enquired.

'Then I'll have made one hell of a mistake,' Chad replied coolly.

'All right, supposing there is air coming in. It may be just a crack it's coming through,' Tom objected.

'That's why I need to go down and take a look. I'll be taking the lamp with me, so don't move about too much up here.'

'Are you sure about this, Chad?' Tom asked anxiously.

'Nope, but Corday's right in what he says. Without food and water, in a few days we'll be joining those coves in the abyss and I'm not giving that jasper the pleasure.' Chad's face hardened. 'I've got other ideas for him and McMurdo and a powerful urge to see them through.'

'You allus was a stubborn cuss, brother,' Tom said without malice.

Chad's first problem was how to get down without breaking the lamp. If it got broken or went out their only source of light was gone. It was Kate who solved the problem. She tore a series of narrow strips from the hem of her skirt and tied them together to form a crude rope. With one end of the rope attached to the handle of the lamp, it could be lowered down from above leaving Chad's hands free for the climb. The idea worked well. With Tom doing the lowering and keeping pace with Chad, Chad reached the bottom in a matter of minutes and untied the lamp, holding it out before him.

Dark, squealing shapes fled from the light, seeking the safety of the shadows. They moved bones as they sought these dark places, filling the abyss with a creak and clatter that raised the small hairs on the nape of Chad's neck. It sounded like the dead were stirring all about him. A cold, clammy sweat broke out over his body and his heartbeat went up a notch or two. Licking dry lips and pushing the fanciful ideas from his mind, he swung the lamp slowly, first to the right and then the left. The movement caused shadows to shorten in the ragged sockets of the grinning skulls, until it appeared as though they too were looking for something. It was in the far left-hand corner that a patch of darkness remained after the rest had fled before the lamp's baleful gaze. It looked like an opening and a surge of excitement pulsed through him. For those watching from above the scene presented an eerie sight with yellow light rising up from the abyss and its awful occupants.

'Can you see anything?' Tom called down.

'Looks to be an opening over yonder.' Chad's voice floated hollowly from the abyss as Tom and Amos followed the direction of his pointing finger. 'I'll take a look.' Chad started forward on a diagonal course that would take him to the opening. His bruised and cut feet brushed against the human remains, the bones feeling like ice. Once he inadvertently stepped on a bone and it exploded with a noisy crack that set his heart thumping. He reached his goal only after clearing a rattling skeleton aside. Cool, dry air fanned his nostrils. He pushed his head and shoulders into the opening, which was roughly circular and some two feet across and extended the lamp. The tunnel he found himself in ran level for a few feet then began a gentle curve upwards. Where it would take them was something they would have to find out for themselves.

Before returning across the abyss, he searched the other walls to see if any other openings existed. He found none. His search to the right took him to where the newer, decomposing bodies lay and closer to the scampering rats, their claws clicking on the stone floor. He tried not to look at the terrible bodies, but only partially succeeded. Twice he felt rats run across his bare feet and his flesh crawled with revulsion. He looked up as he returned to the side of the abyss he had climbed down and saw a pair of pale, anxious faces above the rim.

'What's the verdict, Chad?' Tom called down.

'Looks to be a way to go. Air smells fresh and sweet coming through. Got no guarantee where it's gonna take us, but it's the only chance we've got.'

'I don't think I can do it.' Kate came forward, voice trembling.

'The alternative is Corday and his boys. Don't figure they'll treat you very ladylike, ma'am,' Chad called up.

Amos rose to his feet and gripped his wife's shoulders gently.

'He's right, honey.'

'But the tunnel may not lead anywhere. Become too small. We could get stuck ...'

'Hush, woman.' Amos shook her roughly as he heard panic edge into her voice. 'Ain't no good worrying what might be. Anything's better than staying here and waiting to die.'

'Hey up there,' Chad called. 'As I see it, Corday ain't gonna wait for ever. Sooner or later, when he don't get no answer from us, he's gonna come looking. I reckon that time'll be sooner, so I'd appreciate you folks making up your minds real quick.'

'We're on our way, Chad,' Tom called down and eyed the other two. 'Chad's right and I don't aim to be here when Corday comes looking.' With that Tom slipped over the edge and began the climb down.

'You can do it, honey,' Amos coaxed.

Her eyes searched his face.

'Hold me, Amos. Tight.' For a long minute Amos held his wife's trembling body until she finally struggled free. 'What are we waiting for?' she smiled bravely.

For an hour Garth Corday waited at the mouth of the tunnel. Finally he grew tired of waiting. Hunter had stopped replying to his goading. He had ordered a slave to be kitted out with a coat, hat and empty rifle and the man made to stand in the tunnel entrance. He should have looked enough like a guard to have brought a fusillade of shots from the fugitives. Nothing!

Using a line of slaves as a shield Corday sent some of his men into the tunnel while he remained behind. He did not expect the news that a single, sweating, guard brought back to him.

'What do you mean gone?' There's nowhere to go!' Corday shouted.

'That's as maybe, Mr Corday, but they ain't there,' the man persisted doggedly.

When, finally, Corday himself went into the tunnel, to stand, mouth and nose covered, on the edge of the abyss, he had to admit that somehow the impossible had been achieved. Like his men, he failed to notice the tiny opening in the shadows across the abyss Tom had been the last one to enter and he had had the presence of mind to reach back and drag a skeleton into a sitting position before the opening. It would not have passed close scrutiny, but from the top of the

The Secret of Squaw Mountain

abyss and by lamplight, the opening was concealed.

'How about you tell us what this is all about, Tom. What's McMurdo's game?' Chad asked the question that had been itching at him from the start, but he had not got around to it until now. The four were sprawled about a large, low cave that the narrow tunnel had eventually emerged into. It seemed to have taken a lifetime of crawling on hands and knees and taking the skin off both to get here. Chad had called a halt to rest their aching, weary bodies and chose this moment to ask the question.

Tom, leaning back against the wall, opened his eyes.

'Until McMurdo took on the running of the Squaw mine, it had a steady output. Suddenly the output went up, dramatically up. Almost doubled and with no apparent extra workforce. EM Mines who own the Squaw mine were intrigued. They couldn't understand it and I was sent out to look around. They weren't complaining, you understand, just curious. Maybe McMurdo's methods could be adopted in other mines with the same effect.'

'Some method,' Chad said.

'So I found out to my cost,' Tom replied ruefully.

'I don't figure what McMurdo's getting out of this,' Chad said.

'Neither did I at first until I remembered EM's

bonus scheme. To give managers the incentive to keep costs down, they offered a bonus to any manager able to increase productivity without increasing costs and it was quite a substantial bonus. If I was to tell you that McMurdo has made $10,000 in bonus money in one year you can see what I mean.'

'That's a heap o' money,' Chad commented, impressed.

'And on the surface, all legal,' Tom pointed out bitterly. 'He allows Corday and his men to cream off a little of the gold for themselves to sell through a bogus mine and everyone is happy, unless you happen to end up in the mine doing the digging.'

'Why not take all the extra gold and sell that through the bogus mine?' Amos asked.

'That's where McMurdo is clever. To do that would place him entirely in Corday's hands. The man could take everything and McMurdo would not be able to do a thing. This way everyone gets a bite of the cake and without Corday realizing it, McMurdo has an edge on him. Corday is stealing the gold while McMurdo is being paid. If it came out what was going on at the mine, McMurdo could play the innocent manager. Heap the blame on Corday. After all Corday and his men are the ones responsible for kidnapping travellers to work in the mine. Corday is the one taking the gold and McMurdo would come out of any enquiry as pure as snow. Corday doesn't realize it, but he's the one that will take the blame, if anything goes wrong.'

'And it couldn't happen to a nicer guy,' Chad murmured. 'Well, I reckon McMurdo's gonna be in for a little surprise. Let's get moving.'

Outside the mining office in Grand Mesa, the morning sun baked the main street. Inside, McMurdo raised his own kind of heat as he paced the floor before pausing to glare at a very unhappy Corday.

'Four people do not vanish into thin air,' McMurdo shouted, looking up into Corday's downcast face.

'Well, they did,' Corday insisted sullenly.

'Wrong, Corday. They found a way out that you and your men have missed.'

'We've been over that tunnel inch by inch. The walls are solid,' Corday insisted.

'Have you been down into the pit, the abyss?'

'Well, no, but ...'

'Then it's plain to me that the way they escaped from you and your clowns is to be found in the abyss.'

'I'll get some men down there, but they ain't gonna like it.'

'Would they prefer to end up as the weight on a hangman's noose? Find 'em and get rid of 'em, Corday, before they create more trouble than we can handle.'

'I've got men out looking,' Corday defended himself. 'If they get out of the mine, it won't be easy to reach town. Country all around is pretty flat and any movement would be seen and they ain't exactly dressed for wandering about.' Corday allowed himself a smile.

'Hunter is more resourceful than I gave him credit for,' McMurdo mused. 'If he does slip through your men and get to town ...?' He let the words tail away as he slipped into thought and then a smile filled his face. 'If he gets to town I'll take care of him.'

'How are you gonna do that?' Corday was curious.

'Simple enough. I'm going to get the sheriff to raise a posse. It seems that Mr Hunter is soon to be wanted for the murders of the Wellbeloveds.'

EIGHT

Trasker was leading them deeper into the complex of Squaw Mountain, following ancient trails that at times plunged into narrow canyons and at other times followed narrow ledges that fell sheer on one side to the rocks far below. They had journeyed above the treeline and since dawn had climbed even higher under Trasker's leadership. They were still some way below the snowline, but there was a cool nip in the air.

'How much further, Mr Trasker?' Cora called out.

'Beau, Cora,' Trasker corrected with a smile. 'There's a ways to go yet, but you'll be there come nightfall. We'll stop a spell soon and rest the horses.'

'Must we?' the professor queried impatiently.

'Horses need to rest, sir. 'Sides, that little old canyon city has been there for hundreds of years, so a few more hours ain't gonna matter.'

'I suppose you are right,' the professor grumbled.

'Sure am,' Beau agreed with a laugh.

They entered a flat area some thirty feet across and ringed with large boulders and rock slabs. Amid the rocks a few stunted scrub oak eked out a precarious existence with some withered thorn. Protected by this natural barrier the area within the circle was pleasantly warm.

'Step down folks and take the weight off'n the saddle,' Beau called jovially, swinging from the leatherwork.

Cora gave a sigh of relief. It felt good to stretch her legs. So it was that she was the first to see the Indians. Gathering scrub for a fire to boil the coffee on, the brown, hostile face could have been carved from old wood as it peered at her from the depths of a thorn bush. Only the eyes moving gave away the fact that it was a living, breathing face. She gave a terrified scream and the Indian leapt up, muscles rippling on his smooth-skinned torso, knife gleaming in one brown-fingered hand. He wore hide leggings and moccasins and a leather headband held his long black hair in place.

Cora dropped the armful of scrub and ran towards her father and Trasker. The Indian slithered to a halt, kicking dust. As she reached her father's side the Indian dropped into a menacing half crouch, lips pulled back in a snarling smile.

'Navaho,' Beau said with apparent unconcern.

'What do we do?' the professor hissed, wrapping his arms protectively about Cora as more Indians appeared, spilling over the rock and surrounding the group in a tight circle. They carried flint-headed spears, metal knives and Henrys. They grinned sardonically and gestured at the group with their weapons, causing Cora to whimper with fear.

'Nothing is the best plan,' Beau said breezily.

An Indian pushed his way into the circle. A big man in tan leggings and a flashy red and gold, hand-stitched gambler's vest, open over his broad, scarred chest. His face was weathered and deeply lined. An old scar crossed his left cheek and caught the edge of his mouth, pulling the skin up and giving the face a permanent sneer. He halted before them, dark eyes roaming over Cora, face giving nothing of his thoughts away. He held a Henry in one hand.

'This here's Grey Wolf,' Beau said. 'He's the top man around here. The chief.'

'And these Indians are not dangerous?' The professor sounded worried.

'No, they are my friends,' Beau said and leather creaked as he swung into the saddle, the reins of the other two horses in his hand. ' 'Fraid they ain't your'n though.' He smiled down into two shocked faces.

'I don't understand,' the professor's voice wavered.

'I've done the job McMurdo paid me for,' Beau said and his eyes fell on Cora. 'Pure shame too. Handsome woman like you.' He sighed. 'But business is business.'

'You're working for McMurdo?' Cora could not believe her ears.

'That's about right,' Beau agreed and kneed his horse forward, the other two following. 'You, your pa, the mules. You all belong to Grey Wolf now.'

'You can't leave us like this, Trasker. For pity's sake, man!' the professor implored. 'Get Cora away from here. I'll stay.'

'No, Pa. I'd rather stay with you than go with Mr Trash. Isn't that your name?' she burst out in anger against him and Beau smiled.

'Grey Wolf'll soon knock that sass outta you, girl.' His eyes drifted to the professor. 'Hell no, sir, you won't do at all. For what Grey Wolf's got in mind for Cora you won't do at all.'

Professor Jonas Wellbeloved was not a violent man, but he tried to throw himself at Beau Trasker only to find his path blocked by two spear-carrying Indians.

'Damn you, Trasker, damn you!' the professor shouted.

'Hell, I don't see what you're carrying on for. You'll see your canyon city and meet its only inhabitant, He-with-no-Voice. No, don't thank me yet. Adios, folks. Have a real nice day won't you?'

Laughing, Beau called something to Grey Wolf and the Indian's features split in a huge grin. He eyed Cora and grunted something back as Beau rode away and the Navahos moved in on the two.

Chad was beginning to know how a worm must

feel as the tunnel snaked up, always up, through the rock. By its circular shape and smooth sides, it must have carried water in the long-distant past. The tunnel widened and narrowed. Sometimes, where they hit a patch of soft, porous rock, it widened enough for them to stand in a half crouch. Mostly though, it was on hands and knees and occasionally on stomachs. It was a gruelling, strength-sapping journey and rest periods became more frequent. It was during a rest period that Chad told them about the professor and Cora and the grim news that the two had been tricked onto the mountain to fall into the hands of the Navahos who lived there.

'Heard talk about them Injuns,' Amos brooded darkly. 'Sure don't favour the white man none.'

'Then let's hope we're not too late getting outta this hole.'

'You aimin' to go after this professor and his daughter, Chad?' Tom asked.

'That's the idea,' Chad agreed.

'Half naked, barefooted and with only a few bullets, you intend to take on a whole Navaho tribe?' Tom demanded.

'Does sound kinda foolish,' Chad admitted. 'But that's the general idea.'

Tom shook his head.

'Well, brother, you don't do things by halves do you?' he said.

'When we get out of here, you'll get Kate and Amos off'n this lousy mountain and I'll take care of the other business.'

'When we get out of here, we'll talk about it again,' Tom replied.

They continued their crawl through the never-ending tunnel, knees, elbows and toes scraped raw. Chad had lost all sense of time. Here it was eternal night. He wondered what it was outside. Day or night?

When they stopped for rest again, all were showing signs of exhaustion.

'Sorry, Chad,' Amos gasped. 'Kate's just about had it and I ain't much better. Can't go on.'

'He's right,' Tom broke in. In the gradually waning light of the lamp, both men looked drawn and haggard, faces glistening with sweat. Chad knew they were right, but had been forcing the pace in the hope of getting out before the oil in the lamp ran out. Looking at the flame of the lamp his hope evaporated. The flame was beginning to flicker and pop as it sucked up the last of the oil and could find no more. Kate dragged herself to her husband's side, heedless of the fact that her breasts now hung free, the tatters of her blouse torn away by the constant crawling and hanging in strips. For their part, Chad and Tom tried not to gape and make her feel uncomfortable. They stared silently as the flame dwindled, surged brightly for a few seconds setting shadows dancing over the walls, then died. Darkness enveloped them in silent triumph.

The Secret of Squaw Mountain

* * *

With hands roped before them, Cora and the professor were dragged along like dogs on a lead. All around them the Navahos whooped and called laughing comments to each other. Cora could only guess at their content, but there was no doubt in her mind as to what these gestures meant and her body turned to ice. Fear threatened to burst her heart and formed a choking lump in her throat.

The professor was limping badly on his injured leg and blood now stained the lower part of his pants.

They were led along at a punishing pace and all the time taunted and jeered at. Tears streaked Cora's cheeks as she stumbled over the rough ground, the rope chafing her wrists. She and her father were going to die on Squaw Mountain, thanks to McMurdo and the handsome Texan.

The terrible darkness that followed the lamp going out, enveloped and isolated each within its velvety, black coils. Each could hear the other's breathing. Kate gave a whimper and clutched onto Amos. The darkness could have been a prelude to madness, instead it was a prelude to hope. Chad craned his head around to the direction they were headed and a patch of grey appeared in the darkness ahead. He thought at first that it was just a trick his eyes were playing on him, until he lifted his hand and saw his fingers, black against the grey.

'I can see light ahead,' he called.

'I see it too,' Tom said.

'OK, we move as before. Kate, come towards my voice. I've got my hand out. Feel for it.' Chad heard movement, the fabric of her skirt rasping lightly. Then a hand touched his and fingers fastened. 'I've got you, Kate,' Chad called. 'Amos?'

'Here, Chad.'

'Move until you reach Kate and then Tom, you find Amos.'

'Yo, brother,' Tom called.

When they had linked up and Chad was sure each was facing in the correct direction, he released Kate's hand.

'I'm gonna move forward now. Let's try and keep together.'

As they crawled through the darkness the tunnel narrowed again and it was only Chad, leading, who could see the light. He kept calling back and getting them to answer. The tunnel narrowed to its smallest yet, squeezing in on shoulders and scraping backs.

The light ahead seemed to be getting stronger, but it had no real body to suggest a big opening. The tunnel angled to the right. Chad crawled quickly. The light ahead became a series of white stars and cracks that began to reflect on the tunnel walls. Then hope started to fade as the shutters of despair began to drop in his mind. The light issued between a wall of rocks and boulders that blocked the way ahead. He crawled as far as he could and shouted stop to halt the others.

'What is it?' Tom shouted from the back.

'The way ahead is blocked,' Chad called back, trying to keep the panic and disappointment from his voice. The tunnel was too narrow at this point to turn around. If they had to go back it would mean inching backwards.

'Can you clear it?' Tom asked.

Chad's hands were already ranging over the blockage, probing for weaknesses.

'Ask me again in a few minutes,' Chad grunted back as he exerted pressure at the top.

Stone grated on stone and tiny fragments clattered to the floor of the tunnel. Sweat rolled down Chad's face, stinging his eyes as he pushed as hard as he could. The stone he was pushing at moved inwards and suddenly a finger of light appeared, bright, with the promise of sunlight. Chad renewed his efforts with more frenzy, pushing at the rocks and hearing them tumble down the other side.

As the gap grew more light flooded past him, reaching back as far as Tom. When he judged the gap to be wide enough, Chad hauled himself through and rose up on unsteady legs to find himself in a high, wide cave. From a hole some twenty feet up on the facing wall, almost touching the roof, an angled shaft of sunlight blasted through in a thick, golden bar that hurt the eyes to look at. He turned away and helped a struggling Kate through. Amos and Tom quickly followed and they stood in a tight group, content to just stand and stare for the moment.

'It's been so long that I forgot how good sunlight looks,' Amos breathed, holding Kate to him face shining with happiness. Chad and Tom moved forward, passing either side of the shaft of light to stand beneath the hole and look up. The wall was straight and practically smooth.

'So damn near,' Tom said angrily and pushed a tear from his eye mumbling, 'Dust in my eye.'

Kate and Amos approached.

'Don't look too good eh?' Amos said quietly.

'Take a bit o' pondering,' Chad agreed cautiously.

The four stood there; half naked and dirty, their bodies covered in cuts and scratches, bloodied holes worn in the knees of the pants the men wore. Kate had arranged her tattered blouse as best she could, but it had little covering power now. Her breasts, scratched and grazed around both nipples, stood out proudly. Her nakedness in front of Chad and Tom did not embarrass her. Their eyes did not show the barbaric lust that had glowed in Polecat's.

'Is there a way up?' Kate asked, standing alone with hands on hips. When Chad turned and faced her he couldn't help but admire her figure and unconsciously compared it with Cora's smaller breasted version. He put such thoughts from his mind with a wry smile.

'Don't rightly know yet, ma'am. But I've not

come all this way to fail now.'

It was Amos who provided the answer.

'We make a human ladder,' he said.

'How's that Amos?' Chad asked.

'Like I seen in a circus the one time. One stands at the bottom and the next man stands on his shoulders and the next man stands on the shoulders of the second. The top man should be able to reach the hole and hold on. 'Course those circus fellas, they don't have a wall to lean ag'in, but ...'

'Don't worry 'bout the circus fellas, what comes next?' Tom cut in.

'Well, Kate here climbs the human ladder and gets out. The top man he can now haul himself out,' Amos smiled.

'What about the two left behind?' Tom asked.

'Figure them to wait for the others to get help,' Amos said and Tom looked across at Chad.

'What d'you think, Chad?'

'Idea's good,' Chad agreed. 'Trouble is if anythin' should happen to the two that got out. Remember it's wild country out there. There are the Indians on one hand and McMurdo's men on the other. Finding help is not gonna be easy.'

'Seems it's the only chance we've got,' Tom pointed out.

'Mebbe not,' Chad looked thoughtful, peered up at the hole and back again, rubbing his chin reflectively. It could work! It had to work! He eyed the three. 'With a little variation on the idea we mebbe could all get out.' Three voices asked the same question in unison and Chad held up his hands. 'How we do it is quite simple, the big problem is, *can we do it*. I figure to use Amos's plan to get Kate out. You see I've see'd those circus fellas too, on that trapeze do-dad. One's mebbe holding the other's wrists or ankles and they're swinging about real happy like. Course there ain't no need to swing about here ...'

'Brother, will you say your piece?' Tom howled.

'When Kate's out the man at the top takes a real good hold of the edge of the hole. The one below takes a grip of his ankles and the man at the bottom then climbs up, like Kate did and gets out. When he's out the second man climbs out and finally the top man.'

'If'n he ain't done stretched his arms so long his feet reach the ground,' Tom said.

'Like I said. It won't be easy. Man falls he's likely to do himself a heap o' damage. If'n it works, we're all out together.'

'Who takes what position, Chad?' Amos asked.

Chad eyed Amos and Tom. In height and build they were much the same, Tom a little broader in the shoulder.

'Tom can take bottom. You next, Amos, and I'll take top.'

'Let's give it a try,' Tom said.

'We'll rest a spell. We'll only get the one chance so we've gotta make the most of it,' Chad said.

* * *

The Navaho village, a series of mud and hide wickiups, sprawled untidily at the mouth of a deep canyon that scarred the stone flesh of the Squaw. The area at the mouth of the canyon was flat and possessed a trickling stream that a stand of elm and ash crowded around. The water gave the area an unexpected burst of fertility. In a crude corral, wiry Pintos cropped grass and over to one side a field of corn blazed golden in the sun.

Cora and the professor were surrounded by noisy, half naked children and round-faced women in dark clothing who proceeded to prod and poke at Cora and chatter amongst themselves. Young braves stood at the edge of the circle eyeing Cora, whose hands were still bound. Finally Grey Wolf sent the women and children away with harsh, barked cries. The ropes were cut from their wrists and again they were surrounded by a ring of warriors. Grey Wolf eyed her with his dark, impassive eyes, sending a chill through her body.

'This is an outrage,' the professor spoke up as he rubbed his chafed wrists. 'The American government will send many soldiers.'

'Bluelegs no come onto Squaw,' Grey Wolf said. 'This Navaho land.'

'Men will come looking for us,' Cora said in a shaking voice and a wintry smile cracked Grey Wolf's face.

'Then they will die.' He eyed Cora again. 'Tonight, after the feast of He-with-no-Voice, you will be mine. Learn to be good squaw.'

'No!' Cora shrank back against her father.

'You can't do this,' the professor cried.

'Tonight, old man,' Grey Wolf eyed the professor, 'you will meet He-with-no-Voice. He grows restless with hunger.' He turned away, issuing commands. Cora and the professor were separated and led away. Cora was taken to a domed wickiup and thrust inside. Within the hot, noisome interior she was left on her own to contemplate the terrors of the coming night.

NINE

Kate was out and now Chad hung by both hands hooked over the lower edge of the opening, facing the wall. Below him Amos hung onto his ankles. Now it was Tom's turn to climb the human ladder. Time was at a premium. Strength would drain quickly now. As it was Chad felt as though his arms and legs were being pulled from their sockets. With the two men hanging at arm's length, Tom was able to start from the floor. Going as quickly and carefully as he could, Tom commenced his climb.

Sweat dripped from Amos's face. He grunted as a knee ground into his shoulder. He gripped Chad's ankles so tight that Chad felt as though the bones were being crushed. Amos hung on with grim determination as Tom's weight pressed down on him, threatening to break his hold on Chad's ankles, but finally the weight was gone.

The edge of the opening dug into Chad's fingers, trying to prise the creaking joints apart. As Tom's fingers gouged into his shoulders he began to wonder at the wisdom of his variation on an idea. As Tom used Chad's arms to haul himself higher, his shifting body ground Chad's face into the rock. There was nothing Chad could do but suffer in silence.

Grunting, Tom reached up and gripped the edge of the opening either side of Chad's white fingers and he hauled himself out into the sunlight, a knee smashing unintentionally on Chad's left hand. Now it was Amos's turn. Chad hoped he would hurry up. He felt that his time was limited. Both hands were now alive with a terrible agony and the feeling had left his feet, blood cut off by Amos's grip. He felt Amos moving below him, jerking at his body, stretching tendon and sinew. He grunted as Amos wrapped his arms about his waist. Chad's shoulder joints felt as though hot, ragged-edged knives had been pushed into them.

Amos, breathing harshly, fought to find non-existent toe holds. The sweat that now covered both their bodies helped to lubricate their flesh as Amos hooked a hand over Chad's right shoulder and dragged himself up. Feet dug cruelly into Chad's hips, then a knee ground against the back of his neck. Chad wanted to scream at the awful agony that now clawed at his body. The hiss of blood pumped by his rapidly beating heart filled Chad's ears. Then the awful pressure was gone. Amos was being hauled out by Tom. It was then that Chad realized that he could not move. There was nothing left in his stretched and aching arms

The Secret of Squaw Mountain 117

to haul himself up with and slowly his pain-filled fingers were beginning to uncurl. Taking a deep, shuddering breath, Chad concentrated his failing strength into his uncooperative arms. Sweat ran down his face and dripped onto his chest.

'Only you to go now, Chad.' Chad heard Tom's voice mingled with the hiss of his own blood in his ears. Chad's toes scraped against the rock, one toenail ripping away before he found a tiny ledge to curl his bleeding toes on. He pushed upwards, elbows bending painfully, muscles screaming in agony. He managed to hook an elbow over the edge of the opening and then willing hands slid under his arms. He was hauled out and propped up on a large boulder, unable, for the moment, to open or close his fingers. The others were volubly jubilant over their escape. Chad could only manage a ghastly smile.

'You have some crazy ideas at times, brother,' Tom said. 'I figured we were all goners there, but it worked.'

'Remind me to keep my ideas to myself in the future,' Chad grated out as he flexed his fingers, wincing at the stabs of pain that jabbed at the joints. His feet prickled as the blood returned, but he was elated. He was one step nearer to settling with McMurdo and Corday.

He rose gingerly to his feet and walked forward a few paces, rotating his aching, stiff shoulders as he went. It was at that moment that the Indian came over the rocks, the sun at his back. The four had emerged from the tunnel at the base of a high, splintered crag, before which lay a circular depression some twenty feet across ringed with slabs and boulders. Chad was close to the centre of this circle, the others grouped to one side. Chad's face was to the sun when a shadow passed across his closed lids. His eyes opened in a squint as the Indian's moccasined feet slammed the hard-packed earth before him, sending out puffs of dust.

The dark, round, flat-nosed face below a double eagle-feathered headband, radiated hostility. In the ebony eyes Chad saw that the Indian was mentally, as well as physically, geared up for battle. He was young, probably looking for his first kill. Clad in a hide breech cloth, his muscular legs and chest were bare. In one hand he held a short, flint-tipped lance and in the other, a broad, metal-bladed knife.

Chad clawed at the gun in his waistband, but the hammer snagged in the material. A smile exposed the Indian's teeth and a whooping ululation filled the air as he lunged forward, jabbing with the lance, hair flowing about his face but not covering his eyes. Chad gave up the idea of freeing the gun. He sidestepped, lifting his left arm and the flint head of the lance opened a red flowing cut over his ribs. Heart hammering Chad brought his arm down, trapping the wooden shaft of the lance against the side of his body. At the same time he brought his right hand across, gripping the shaft as he swivelled his body to the left. The move snatched the lance from the Indian's hand. Making it seem a continuation of the same move, Chad brought his right leg up as he pivoted back on his left leg, then he kicked out with the right foot, the bare sole catching the surprised Indian high on the chest.

The Indian staggered back against the rocks, throwing his arms out sideways to break the fall. He was in this spread-eagled position, still clutching the knife, when Chad ran forward and thrust, double-handed, with the lance. It entered the Indian's stomach just above the navel, slicing and tearing through the intestines with such force that the flint head emerged from the Indian's back just right of the spinal column and grated on stone.

With a gurgling shriek of agony that sprayed red into the air, the Indian dropped the knife and grabbed at the wooden shaft protruding from his body. Blood flowed from the jagged hole made by the flint head. It covered the shaft and turned his hands a glistening red. Blood ran from the Indian's mouth and splashed onto his heaving chest. It ran down his legs in multiple streams, pooling in the dust as he staggered forward and sank to his knees. His glazing eyes had time for one last hate-filled stare at Chad, before they seemed to look through him. He fell forward onto the lance he still gripped. His weight pushed the lance deeper into his body, causing the bloody, intestine-strung, flint head to emerge further before he toppled sideways and lay still in a widening pool of blood.

Chad had no time to review the situation. A gun spoke, jerking his eyes from the corpse as the sound rattled about the stone clearing. He was in time to see a second Indian, Navaho like the first, tumble from the rocks above and crash down at Tom's feet. Smoke drifted from the barrel of Tom's gun. Chad freed his gun, thumbing the hammer back in readiness, eyes searching the rocks as he moved back to the others. Amos stood protectively before Kate, face set.

'Let's get out of here,' Chad said urgently and led them in a scramble over the rocks to drop down onto a slope that angled steeply to a wall of trees below. Behind them the rocks made up part of a long escarpment of stone that stretched away into the distance, following the top of the slope.

'Which way?' Tom called.

'Make for the trees,' Chad replied. 'We need to find cover before their friends turn up.' They were halfway down the slope when Chad slithered to a halt, his keen eyes picking out movement on the edge of the trees towards which they were headed. 'Indians!'

Tom had already seen them. 'Three I make it.'

'Up there, more,' Kate shouted, pointing to the escarpment above. Four more Indians were outlined against the cobalt sky. Neither group made any attempt to attack them even though they carried Henrys. Now that they had stopped, so had the Indians.

'What do we do, Chad?' Amos asked.

'Follow the slope around.'

As they moved off again, in single file, so the Indians moved, keeping pace with them.

'What are they waiting for?' Tom called to Chad.

'I guess we'll find out soon enough,' Chad replied, equally puzzled by the Indians' behaviour. They were Navahos and must have found their dead brothers, but still they did not attack. Chad had the uncomfortable feeling that the Indians wanted them to go this way. Ten minutes later he found out why.

The ground underfoot was bare rock, heated by the sun to foot-blistering intensity. It radiated heat in shimmering waves and forced the moisture from their bodies. As the slope curved, a line of thin straggling trees appeared ahead that marched up the slope and marked the edge of a wide gorge. Fifty or sixty feet below them white water churned and boiled angrily as it raced through the gorge. Above its roar came a heavier, deeper rumble that Chad recognized as a waterfall, and a big one by the sound of it. It lay somewhere to the left, hidden from sight by the bend in the gorge. The walls of the gorge were sheer and Chad realized with cold dismay that they were trapped.

'End of the line,' Tom murmured dully as he stared down at the water.

Chad looked around for the Indians, but they

were nowhere to be seen.

'Well this is where we make our stand,' Chad declared unhappily. 'You folks check your guns. Let's see what sort of fight we can make.' Tom had four bullets, Amos six, Kate two and Chad three. Chad grinned wryly. 'Looks like it's only gonna be a short one. Take cover. Got nothing to do now but wait.'

There were a series of low outcroppings that puckered the edge of the gorge like wrinkles around an old scar. The four spread themselves out behind them to wait.

It was not a long wait!

A bullet threw rock splinters and dust into Chad's face as he peered cautiously over the rock before it screamed away into the sky. Chad rolled aside, cursing and rubbing his stinging, watering eyes. More shots came from a different direction. Chad only half saw the Indian rise from behind a scrub bush less than ten feet to his left on the edge of the gorge. The Indian was a blur in his still watery vision as he brought up his gun and fired. The Indian jerked, the rifle spinning from his hands to disappear into the gorge, then fell, a bullet through his heart.

Bullets were coming in from all directions now as Chad cleared his vision. Tom and Amos were firing back at unseen targets.

'Don't shoot unless you can see 'em clear!' Chad shouted at them.

A lance bounced off the rocks and sailed over

The Secret of Squaw Mountain

Chad's head. A figure loomed. Chad snapped a shot, but missed. The Indians were playing with them, making them use up their meagre supply of ammunition. The sound of the gunshots fled down the slope, bullets giving out their keening cry as they ricocheted into the air. Chad knew that they were fighting a battle they could not win.

Tom gave a cry, the gun flying from his grasp as he grabbed at his shoulder, blood spurting between his fingers. Chad crawled across.

'Tom?'

'I'm OK, flesh wound,' Tom gasped out, face ashen and creased in pain.

Yelling, an Indian launched himself over the rock at Amos. Amos did not have time to bring his weapon to bear before the Indian was on him. Chad tried to get a clear shot only to have the shaft of a lance smash down onto his gun wrist. The gun fell from Chad's hand as his wrist went numb. Chad's attacker came in, knife-blade flashing. Chad threw himself onto his back and kicked up between the Indian's legs. The man gave an agonized howl as he doubled up, clutching himself between the legs. Chad came to his feet as the Indian launched himself forward, face still laced with pain. Chad caught the knife wrist and in turn had his other wrist held by the Indian and the two stood locked together, chest to chest in a trial of strength.

In the meantime all shooting had now stopped as the Indians swarmed over the rocks. Amos lay unconscious, blood welling from a cut on his forehead. Tom was on his knees, arms twisted behind his back by one Indian as a second bound his wrists with a rawhide thong. Kate had the attention of the remaining three. They seemed to have forgotten the fighting and were concentrating on stripping the ragged clothing from her body as she was held against a rock. Dark hands kneaded her breasts and dark eyes grew lustful. She screamed in despair as she was stripped naked and her legs forced apart.

Chad could hear her screams as he fought against the strength of the Indian. Chad's face showed the strain and a pulse beat in his temple. Kate's screams tortured his ears as the Indian's greater strength began to tell. The Indian grinned and then savagely butted his head into Chad's face. Chad heard bone crunch in his nose and a flood of hot blood flowed over his lips. Pain lanced behind his eyes as the Indian jerked his knife wrist free, but retained his grip on Chad's wrist.

Chad shook his head to clear it. Blood, his own, stained his sweating chest in a gory, red blanket. By now Kate's screams had dropped to tiny, mewing whimpers as her attackers were joined by the two who had tied Tom. Tom himself lay slumped against a tree bole. The Indians surrounding Kate completely hid her from Chad's eyes, but by the taunts and jeers the Indians batted about, there was no doubt what was going on. There was also no doubt what was going to happen to him. His attacker was anxious to get in on the fun with a white woman. He brought the knife up in a disembowelling thrust. Chad blocked the blow, knocking it aside and driving a fist against a rock-hard muscle layer that covered the Indian's stomach. It did nothing but make the Indian grunt.

The Indian released his grip and sprang away to face Chad in a half crouch. Chad staggered back. His nose, blue and swollen, throbbed painfully. He wiped blood from his lips and glared at the man through blackening eyes.

'Come on, dog-shit warrior. See if'n you can take a real man,' Chad invited. He was not sure if the man could speak his lingo or if he just guessed the rough content of Chad's words. With a snarl he threw himself at Chad. Chad tried to get out of the way, but his foot snagged a rock. The Indian hit Chad and both men went down. Chad had forgotten the gorge until he found himself hanging over the edge, with nothing but air beneath his shoulders. The Indian, in his anger, had also forgotten it until now. His eyes widened as he sat astride Chad's middle. He tried to stab down with the knife but Chad caught his wrist again. This time Chad bunched his right fist and slammed it hard into the Indian's face. He had the satisfaction of seeing the Navaho's lips mash and split, before the man fell forward to smother the blows. The move was a mistake on the Navaho's part. The balance of weight shifted and Chad felt himself toppling and the cold hand of fear clutched his heart in an iron grip. The Indian tried to scramble back, but Chad caught his hair.

'Let's go to hell together, boy,' he said and both men fell.

Tom saw his brother and the Indian disappear and a great weight settled over his heart. The Indians left Kate sprawled inelegantly over the rock as they rushed to the edge. She let her battered, defiled body slide to the ground. She had not seen what had happened, all she wanted to do was find a hole and crawl into it.

Chad hit the water. The Indian hit a rock that broke his spine and shattered his ribs, the force of the fall pushing splintered bones through the skin in bloody destruction. For an instant he lay there, then the water gathered him up and whirled him away.

As soon as Chad plunged beneath the seething, white surface, cross-currents tore at his body, spinning and rolling him this way and that, dragging him down into secret depths that were more treacherous than the surface. Dazed and disorientated, buffeted by the currents, he was whirled away with no idea which way was up or which way was down. The air he had taken in on the way down was all but used up now and his lungs felt as though they were on fire.

Water was beginning to syphon down the back of his throat through his nose when he was swept into a shallow. His head broke the surface and he dragged air into his lungs. The merciless water played a spiteful game with him, turning him over, scraping his shoulders along the bottom.

The sound of the river, roaring and hissing all around him, filled his ears. Far above him the sky was a twisting blue line that followed the curve of the gorge. The deeper rumbling was louder now, a deep, ominous drumming of awesome power. The turbulent river plunged him between black, glistening boulders that raised white feathers of spray into the air. He hit his left shoulder as he was squeezed between rocks, then he was clear of the white water and being carried along on a surface of black. He tried to fight the current, but his battered body refused to respond.

The drumming rumble grew louder. Ahead hung a cloud of white spray strung across the gorge like a huge, dusty, glowing cobweb as the sun struck it, while arching above the spray was a rainbow of pure, vibrant colours. Under normal circumstances Chad would have found great beauty in the sight, but now it filled him with dread, for it marked the falls he had heard for so long and not yet seen. If sound was an indication of size, then these were enormous.

Spray enveloped Chad in a grey cocoon as the river reached the edge of its world and he was thrown into space. Chad burst through the cloud to see below him a huge wall of white plunging sheer to a maelstrom of black, spinning water that clouds of spray drifted lazily across. Chad felt himself dropping against the curtain of white towards the dark, awesome vortex that beckoned him. The voice of the waterfall rose up to meet him, deep and thunderous as it beat into his brain. For a few seconds he seemed to be hanging motionless in the air looking down onto the world. The next minute he struck the water and became part of that world as he was sucked down and down, knowing that if he should hit the bottom his frail body would be reduced to a boneless pulp.

He flailed about with arms and legs, in an attempt to slow his descent, barely conscious as the light vanished, leaving him in a roaring blackness as he was dragged deeper and deeper into the deadly heart of the vortex; dragged to his death.

TEN

Cora had not been touched since being thrown into the smelly, domed hut. She had sat and wept and listened to the sounds that floated in from outside. It was the ordinariness of the sounds that struck her. Children laughing and shouting as they played games. A dog barking. Nothing to indicate the savagery that existed. She wondered what had happened to her father. Was he imprisoned in a manner similar to hers?

She sat, knees drawn up, in the centre of the hut. A number of animal skins had once covered the dirt, these were now piled to one side for they were alive with bugs and insects. On her own she had nothing to do but contemplate the miserable existence that awaited her. How long she had been in the hut she had no way of knowing, it seemed like for ever, when a commotion from outside brought her to her feet, fear catching in her throat as she backed away from the entrance flap.

Light sprang through the entrance as the flap

was lifted. Fierce eyes glared at her as two Navaho men entered carrying something between them. It was only when they threw Kate unceremoniously to the ground that Cora realized the naked figure was a white woman. The men withdrew and Cora went hesitantly forward. The figure seemed so still, huddled on its side, back towards her, that Cora feared she was dead. Then the figure rolled onto her back and eyes flickered open.

'Water!' Kate could barely get the word out from a throat that was as dry as a bone. Being made to run and scramble behind horses, wrists tied, had left her weak and exhausted. Her feet made Cora gasp out in mixed horror and revulsion. The harsh terrain had reduced them to bloody ruins. Kate had to repeat the request before Cora snapped out of the trance and brought an earthenware jug of brackish water, its surface coated in a layer of dead flies and insects, to Kate's side.

After scraping the surface clean with one hand Cora managed to trickle water from the jug into Kate's mouth. The warm, brackish water tasted like pure nectar to Kate. Later, Cora shook out one of the skins, flesh crawling at the insects that fell from it, and laid it out for Kate. She had poured water over Kate's torn and lacerated feet. It was all she could do. Afterwards she found the woman eyeing her strangely, propped up on her elbows, impervious to her nakedness. Ignoring it. Proper introductions had not been passed

The Secret of Squaw Mountain 131

between the two, so Cora was mystified when Kate said.

'You must be Cora Wellbeloved?'

Cora stared at her in fascination.

'How could you know that?'

Kate smiled and eased herself back down again to lie full length on the skin. After telling Cora her name she launched into the story of the mine and a man called Chad Hunter who had made their escape possible. Cora listened with growing horror that turned to dismay and grief.

'Chad's dead?' Cora whispered after Kate had talked herself out. She didn't want to believe it. The only thing that had kept her going since the capture was the thought that maybe, somehow, Chad would find them. Now that hope was gone.

Kate looked up into the distraught face of the kneeling girl.

'Tom saw him fall into the gorge. He meant something special to you?'

Cora nodded dumbly, fighting back the tears, and told Kate her own story.

Outside, the hot afternoon sun beating down on them, Amos and Tom hung limply against the rawhide thongs that bound them upright to thick posts driven into the ground. They provided a centrepiece in the Indian village for the curious and hostile to come and stare at or shout taunts at. Neither man had been given water. Amos was unconscious, Tom almost.

Professor Wellbeloved sat alone in a guarded

dwelling on the other side of the village to Cora. He sat on a skin, heedless of the beetles that scuttled about. In his lap he cradled two earthenware pots. One was badly chipped, the other in perfect condition. He was almost oblivious to the danger he faced at the hands of the Navahos as he endlessly studied the pots that the Navaho appeared to be using for everyday purposes. They were Anasazi pots and somewhere, close by, must be the Anasazi city. If only he could see it.

As he sagged in his bonds, Tom became the target for a group of stone-throwing children while the adults looked on approvingly. Blood was already trickling from a stone cut above his right eye and he gasped as a big stone crashed against his ribs. He began to envy Chad his death in the rushing waters of the gorge. At least it would have been over quickly.

In that, Tom was wrong. Chad Hunter was not a man to take kindly to death. He fought it every inch of the way, a deep-seated, subconscious reaction to the violent life he led. As the others, at the top of the gorge, were being led away on rawhide ropes behind Indian ponies, Chad looked far from alive as he dragged himself from a tranquil pool beyond the vortex that swirled below the waterfall. Inch by painful inch Chad dragged himself up a grassy slope beneath a cooling canopy of trees. The rumble of the falls still rang

The Secret of Squaw Mountain

in his ears, but this time it was not a death knell it was tolling.

Chad lay there, half in, half out of the water, sucking air into his lungs and trying to bring his shaking body under control. He could not make out why he was not dead. His body felt bruised and battered, as though he had just been run over by a herd of stampeding cattle.

As his strength slowly returned he dragged himself clear of the water and, with the use of a nearby tree, hauled himself to his feet. As he stood there, back against the rough bark, his thoughts focused on the plight of Kate, Amos and Tom. Were they alive or dead? Prisoners of the Navaho or food for the buzzards? Then there was Cora and the professor, what of them? The answer to everything lay in the Navaho village that he somehow had to find.

He looked around. Before him lay the huge pool, a thick mesh of trees spreading around its sides until they met the towering ramparts of the cliff and its curtain of ceaselessly tumbling water. As he gazed to the right his heart jumped in his chest. Amid some stones and lush grass, a brown hand, fingers partially clasped, jutted up. There was no movement from the hand. Chad stole forward, heart hammering in his chest and his expression became one of horror as he stared down into a tiny inlet carved into the riverbank. Here, snagged on some tree roots, lay the broken, shattered remains of an Indian, probably the one he had been fighting when both had fallen into the gorge. He was an example of how not to do it. With an eye to the practical, Chad set about removing the dead man's moccasins and pulling them on his own feet. They were a little tight, but better than nothing. It made Chad feel better as he moved through the forest that skirted the pool, heading for the higher slopes where he hoped to find the Navahos, providing they didn't find him first, half naked and unarmed. He didn't have much going for him, but maybe that was the edge he needed.

It was the fire that brought Chad to the Navaho village. From a high pass with the cool night wind scratching coldly at his bare flesh, Chad had seen the fire; a distant, flickering beacon in the blackness that surrounded him.

He had returned to the top of the gorge, a journey that took him well into the afternoon, and from there followed the tracks. Many ponies and three people walking on bloodstained feet. He had dined earlier on fruits and berries he had found in the forest, the sweetness in them giving him the energy he needed for the long pursuit. The tracks had not been hard to follow, but it was time that was against him. Night came all too quickly, hiding the tracks. He had almost prepared himself to camp for the night amid the rocks when he saw the fire. It took him almost two hours, but finally he reached the village.

The city had been built beneath a huge overhang

in the canyon wall. Stone dwellings that rose on a series of terraces, disappearing back into the darkness beneath the overhang. As the sun was setting, filling the canyon with misty, purple shadows, Professor Wellbeloved was brought from the village. His eyes widened as he saw the silent, long-deserted city. Fingers of red painted the upper reaches of the canyon wall a lurid scarlet and touched the walls of the highest stone buildings.

He paid scarce attention as he was tied, in a standing position, with strips of rawhide, between two short, thick posts. Held by the wrists, the lengths of rawhide were not long enough to allow him to bring his hands together, but did allow a certain amount of body movement.

The strip of red painting the upper canyon wall rapidly grew thinner as the sun sank lower and the Anasazi city faded in the darkness that rose from the canyon floor. All around the purple shadows were deepening. Grey Wolf stepped before the professor. Behind the Navaho leader, four braves stood holding flaming brush torches.

'Soon He-with-no-Voice will come and the Great Spirit will be avenged against the unbelievers that dare to climb the sacred Mountain,' he intoned darkly.

'What do you mean?' the professor queried nervously as he became aware of the reality of the situation and tugged at his bonds. Grey Wolf merely smiled. He made a sign to the torch bearers who moved to the four corners of an imaginary square around the professor, thrust the ends of the torches into the sandy ground and withdrew to behind Grey Wolf. Flickering shadows licked over the group as darkness from above fell to join that rising from the canyon.

'To light your way to death,' Grey Wolf said and, with his braves, melted into the darkness leaving the professor on his own.

The flames from the fire cast a lurid glow over the dwellings of the village, sending dancing shadows beween the wickiups. The men of the tribe, about fifty, sat in a circle around the fire gorging on fish and game and drinking from the bottles of whiskey supplied by Beau Trasker in the supplies that, unknown to the Wellbeloveds, the pack mules had carried. The women and children were consigned to a smaller fire and a single drum beat out a monotonous rhythm.

From his position on the edge of the village, the smell of meat bubbling in its own juices made Chad's mouth water. He put the thought of food aside as Cora and Kate were led into the circle. Cora was forced to sit beside a big, imposing Indian that Chad took to be Grey Wolf. Kate, naked, was made to stand beween the men and the fire. The way she moved and the grey pain that etched her face, told Chad that her feet were in a bad way. They were not helped any as a young Indian, whiskey bottle in one hand, leapt

The Secret of Squaw Mountain 137

up, grabbed a handful of Kate's hair and began to stroll briskly around the fire. Kate screamed in agony as she was forced to walk on swollen, bleeding feet around the circle of drunken, jeering Indians. It angered Amos who began to shout curses at the Indians until two braves leapt up and clubbed him into silence. Tom remained silent, head bowed. Chad could not see the professor anywhere and he had to find him before he could do anything else.

He found the professor twenty minutes later and studied him cautiously from a stand of cedar that fringed one side of the canyon. He waited in silence, unable to detect any guards nearby. He was about to make a move towards the tethered man when the cold, hard end of a rifle barrel pressed against the side of his neck.

'White eyes!' came a snarling voice.

Chad rose slowly to his feet, arms raised, and turned to face the man who had managed to creep up on him. In the faint touch of the brush torches, a silly smile wreathed the Indian's face and he swayed a little from side to side. Whiskey breath fanned over Chad.

'Leaping Deer see white eyes. Leaping Deer catch white eyes,' he boasted.

'Good for Leaping Deer,' Chad murmured.

Movement came from Chad's left, stealthy, heavy movement and a look of fear filled the Indian's eyes.

'He-with-no-Voice comes.' There was a pathetic,

supernatural dread in the Indian's voice. His eyes wavered in the direction of the sounds that grew more disturbed and violent. Chad saw his chance and leapt forward, wrenching the rifle barrel to one side and kicking into the Indian's stomach. The man doubled up with a groan, releasing his grip on the rifle and sinking to his knees, vomiting whiskey and meat.

The violent rustling of the undergrowth ceased. Whatever it was had emerged from the trees. Chad peered out. Something huge and black sped towards the torch-lit figure. It was only as it got to within ten feet of the tethered man, that it rose on stumpy hindlegs into the shape of a huge, black grizzly bear. As it reared before the professor the terrified man gave a yell and drew himself as far back as the rawhide thongs would let him.

The beast's muzzle gaped, but no sound came out. It waved its front paws and took a few steps forward. Glistening strings of saliva hung from its jaws. Chad threw up the rifle, then changed his mind. A shot would bring the village running. Instead he turned on the still groaning Indian, hauled him to his feet by his hair and dragged him in his wake towards the bear and its intended victim.

The Indian pulled a knife and Chad wasted precious seconds, disarming the man with a rifle butt to the face. The man went down, screaming hoarsely as his cheekbones shattered. The bear turned, **sensing the two. In the flickering** torchlight Chad could see that one side of its throat was badly scarred. That was probably the reason for its silence, its vocal chords were damaged. Chad yelled at it and hauled the Indian to his feet. As the bear turned towards them Chad sent the man staggering forward into the creature's path.

A hideous scream ripped the air as the bear engulfed the Indian in a crushing hug. Chad retrieved the knife and darted to the professor's side, slashing the rawhide bindings. Behind him the Indian's screams stopped abruptly as the bear's jaws fastened on his face and bone crunched sickeningly beneath the sharp teeth.

In the village the drumming stopped and heads canted on one side to hear the thin, terrified screams issuing from the canyon. When the screams ceased Grey Wolf rose to his feet and raised both hands above his head in victory. From the throats of the gathered throng rose a wild cheer followed by laughter and bottles raised. Grey Wolf dropped down beside Cora.

'He-with-no-Voice has taken the old man,' he grunted and saw Cora's face whiten and sag. He gripped her chin roughly and turned her head to his. 'This is no place for sadness. Drink!' He pushed a bottle towards her. She jerked her head free and looked away as tears welled in her eyes. Grey Wolf laughed loudly and sucked on the bottle neck. It was five minutes later that a wickiup on the far edge of the village burst into flame. By the time it registered on the drunken men, a second one caught fire.

With the professor in tow, Chad, with a torch taken from the canyon, began to systematically fire the outer wickiups, running from one to the other. Confusion reigned as billows of smoke rolled across the central area in choking swirl. Chad was nearing where Tom and Amos were tied when an Indian lurched out in front of him. Chad pushed the torch into the man's startled face and grimaced as the man's long hair blazed, turning him into a human candle. As the man went onto his knees, screaming, Chad tossed the torch onto the last wickiup and clubbed the man into unconsciousness.

Using the billowing smoke clouds as cover Chad reached Tom and slashed the bindings holding him. He did the same to Amos and both men fell to the ground, unable to support themselves. Chad brushed tears from his stinging eyes.

'How the hell?' Tom croaked.

'I'll tell you later,' Chad said as he swung the rifle on a figure emerging from the smoke and fired. The Indian dropped, half his face shot away. Chad helped Tom to his feet. 'Get his gun and knife and moccasins. I'm going for the women.'

Tom had little chance to say anything as Chad vanished into the drifting smoke.

Grey Wolf was on his feet, holding a struggling Cora by the arm and barking gruff commands to his bemused people, when Chad appeared. By

The Secret of Squaw Mountain 141

now one half of the village was ablaze, the drifting smoke clouds tinged orange. Grey Wolf had heard the shots above the crackle of the blazing wickiups and his own yelling, screaming people and a sixth sense told him that what was happening was no accident. As he saw Chad a snarl ripped his lips back from his teeth. He sent Cora sprawling with a shove and swung the rifle, a Winchester, up. The shot that followed came from Chad's gun. The bullet hit Grey Wolf in the throat with devastating effect. It blew the man's head from his neck, jetting blood from the severed arteries. The headless corpse jerked like a puppet in the hands of a spiteful child before crashing to the ground. Chad presumed that the bullets in his rifle had been notched to give greater destruction on impact. They had certainly worked. He tossed the Henry aside in favour of the Winchester and helped a shaking Cora to her feet.

'Chad?' She spoke as though talking to a ghost. 'I thought you were dead!'

'Kinda felt that way at one time,' Chad admitted.

'Chad!' Cora repeated and flung her arms about his neck, kissing him hard on the lips. Chad had to push her away.

'Steady, girl. We're not out of here yet.'

'Cora!' The professor limped into view with Tom and Amos. Tom had got a rifle from somewhere.

'Pa!'

A scream hit their ears. Near to the ceremonial

fire an Indian brave stood over the prostrate form of Kate, lance raised in readiness to plunge it into her body. Two rifles exploded as one. The Indian spun away from Kate, the lance flying from his hands, his intestines hanging in pink and white coils from the gaping hole left by two bullets emerging. The Indian tottered towards the fire, hands grabbing for his exposed insides, and toppled into the fire.

Chad and Tom exchanged glances, then Chad ran forward and lifted Kate in his arms. Her body was spattered with the Indian's blood, but she was laughing and crying as she clung to Chad. Returning to the others Chad passed Kate to Amos.

'Let's get the hell outta here!' Chad shouted and led them to the corral where the ponies moved restlessly to and fro, whinnying their unease at the scent of smoke and fire. On the way to the corral, Chad paused at an empty wickiup, grabbed a blanket and threw it over Kate. At the corral he caught a pony for each of them before letting the rest go. Minutes later, each riding bareback and holding onto their animal's mane, Chad led them from the burning village and into the cool, starlit night.

ELEVEN

The man on the escarpment stiffened and squinted out across the muddy, yellow plain scattered with clumps of dry, green brush and the occasional oak stand, shading his eyes with his hat. He blinked and stared again across the heat shimmering plain and his heart began to beat a little faster. He was right, riders were coming. He waited, peering into the shimmering distance until he could count them before moving back along the escarpment to look down into a long, rectangular box canyon, towards the wooden stockade of the EM Mining Company, Squaw Mountain Division. He waved his hat back and forth until a lookout responded, then he raised his arm ten times to indicate the number before returning to his former position, checking his rifle and hunkering down to watch and wait.

In the office hut, McMurdo received the news of the ten approaching riders with a spasm of unease.

'This is your doing, Corday,' McMurdo accused

angrily. 'Letting Hunter escape.'

'I hear the Wellbeloveds are back,' Corday replied evenly. 'Seems your Navahos couldn't handle them.'

Both men sniped at each other in the heat of the room as the tension built. As soon as McMurdo heard of Hunter's amazing reappearance in Grand Mesa along with the Wellbeloveds and three former slave workers, he had got out of town fast and made his way to the mine. Here he felt safe surrounded by armed men and the stout gates of the stockade plus the barbed wire gates that closed off the mouth of the canyon. He had expected Hunter to come alone and the thought of ten men worried him.

'The men know what to do?' McMurdo questioned nervously and Corday smiled thinly.

'With what you're paying them, those boys are up and raring to go.'

Out on the plain, Sheriff Roy Cooper sweated as he rode beside Chad Hunter. Behind the two, eight more riders rode in a loose group.

'We should get the army for this,' the sheriff opined nervously. Sweat rolled down his face and darkly patched the armpit of his brown shirt beneath a black, leather vest.

'You didn't have to come, Sheriff,' Chad pointed out softly and the sheriff threw him a worried look. He wouldn't have come, but as the story of what was happening at the mine went around town, kin of those who had lost folk in supposed

Indian raids demanded to form a posse and Cooper had no choice but to lead them. He had been all set to arrest Hunter if ever he set foot in Grand Mesa again, until he found out that Hunter's supposed victims were alive and the story they, and those with them, had to tell was so fantastic it had to be true.

'This is the law's business. Man breaks the law around here, he has to pay,' Cooper replied loftily.

'That's how I feel, Sheriff. McMurdo and Corday have to pay,' Chad agreed.

Cooper cast a second glance at Hunter and shivered.

It was a different Chad Hunter from the ragged, half naked rider who had ridden with five others down main street in the cold, half light of dawn. A different Chad Hunter who had ridden into Grand Mesa looking for his brother. The taciturn man, clad in black save for a light blue bandanna at his throat, was death. He wore a pair of black-handled, Colt Frontiers strapped low on each leg, while across his shoulders a specially made harness held a sawn-off, double-barrelled shotgun. The harness was designed to allow the butt of the shotgun to rear at an angle above his left shoulder. He could cross-draw it with his right hand and bring it into play in the blink of an eye. There had been hard men in the past who thought he would not be fast enough. They were dead now. He rode astride a bay mare, until he found his Appaloosa again. The black garb and weapons were the remains of a distant memory that he carried with him, refusing to get rid of them. For ten years the past and present had been separate; now they were one.

Chad had left behind a confused and frightened girl and an angry brother in Grand Mesa. Cora had been there when Chad entered, clad in his all-black garb. She had seen the look of anger and dismay fill Tom's face.

'You can't do it, Chad,' Tom burst out. '*He* died years ago. You promised.' There was a reproachful note in his voice as he stood there, one arm in a sling.

'I made a mistake. Man can't hide from what he is or what he does best or look the other way when there are men like McMurdo and Corday on the prod. I spent ten years trying. It's time for the dead to rise.'

'It's up to the law to take care of it now,' Tom pointed out hotly and a bleak, sour smile tugged at Chad's lips.

'A man like McMurdo can buy the law.'

'But with all the evidence we have. Witnesses, you and I included, he can't get away.'

'It takes time to bring a man like McMurdo to justice. Time for him to get rid of the witnesses. With Corday and his gunsels he has the guns to do it. City law don't work out here, Tom.'

'Please, Chad,' Tom implored.

'I didn't start this fight, Tom. The folks forced to work in that damn mine didn't start it, but I aim

The Secret of Squaw Mountain 147

to finish it,' Chad said grimly.

'Supposing *IT* finishes you?' Tom challenged.

'Then you can try it your way, brother,' Chad replied softly and turned away, heading for the door.

'Look after yourself, Chad,' Tom called and Chad looked back at his brother, a half smile on his face.

'That's what I'm doing.'

Cora had seen the confrontation between the brothers. She did not profess to understand it, feeling that there was something in the conversation that had not been said, that *HE* and Chad were the same person. She followed him out into the shadowy hallway.

'I don't understand what's going on, Chad, between you and Tom, but please come back.' Her voice faltered and she was glad of the gloom that hid the tears that sprang unbidden to her eyes. She leaned up and kissed his lips, soft at first, then harder, before breaking away in confusion and running to her room. She knew in her heart that any dreams she had for the future would not include Chad. The touch of her lips still lingered on Chad's lips, even now.

Two hard looking men wearing mining security stars stood grim-faced behind the locked gates of barbed wire and chicken mesh that closed off the canyon mouth, staring with expressionless eyes at the posse.

'Open up,' the sheriff called. 'We're here to see McMurdo.'

'Can't do that, Sheriff. We'uns got orders,' one of the two said gruffly. They both toted Winchesters loosely in their hands.

'This is official law business,' the sheriff said pompously.

'We're the law here, Sheriff. This mine's outta your jurisdiction.' The man stressed the final word, relishing it and savouring it.

'But it's not out of mine, friend,' Chad spoke up, tired of the back and forth wordplay. He held the sawn-off shotgun in his hands. His eyes were as cold as his voice was bleak. 'You've gotta choice. You open the gates or you die. I don't know how much you and your buddy are getting paid to die, but it sure ain't worth it. And if'n your pal up top figures on using that rifle, we'll be going to hell together.'

The heads of the posse craned up, seeing for the first time the man perched with the rifle above. The speaker licked suddenly dry lips. The man in black was the one who had killed Indios.

'Evans,' he bawled. 'Put up the rifle, they're coming in.' After a moment's hesitation the man complied. 'Ain't no need to shoot, mister.' With the gate being a mere framework to which the barbed wire and chicken mesh were nailed, it offered little protection from the shotgun.

'Toss the guns, gents, and open the gates.'

'Hell, why not?' The man came forward with a

key. 'A fart'd blow these gates down. Don't figure on getting myself killed over these damn gates.' The man opened the gates up as he finished.

'You're getting smart,' Chad approved bleakly. 'Now get real smart and ride outta here while you can.'

The two men eyed each other, nodded and went to their horses. The speaker paused and looked back.

'What about our guns, mister?'

'You're getting outta here with your lives, mister. Be thankful for that.' Chad waited until the two men had ridden off before eyeing the sheriff. 'That was the easy part, Sheriff. The next part is the dying part.' He raised his voice. 'Any of you men having second thoughts, turn back now. You can't change your mind with a bullet in your brain.' There were no dissenters. The sheriff would have liked to, but he didn't get the choice.

McMurdo and Corday joined the man on the lookout platform over the big double gates of the stockade, when it was known that the riders were through the canyon gates.

'Sheriff's joined with Hunter an' they got a regular posse backing them,' Corday said unnecessarily to McMurdo.

'Are your men in place?' McMurdo answered.

'Stationed in the rocks,' Corday said, his eyes never leaving the riders as they came to a halt.

'Let's hope they are better than the two at the

canyon gates.' He raised his voice. 'What brings you here, Sheriff?'

'Seems like we got a problem, Mr McMurdo. Figure a looksee in yonder mine could clear it up pronto,' Cooper called back.

'Only problem we got is that you're trespassing.'

'The law don't trespass, Mr McMurdo.'

'Coming uninvited onto mining land, it does. You got no rights here, unless you got a legal signed warrant. Have you got that, Sheriff?'

Cooper looked uneasy and shifted in his saddle.

'Trying to keep it friendly, Mr McMurdo. Just a look in the mine and there won't be no need for unpleasantness.'

'You need permission from the owners for that, Sheriff, or I'm in legal right to use force to protect the mine. Could be a trick you're playing to get in and steal the gold. Gotta protect it.' McMurdo suddenly sounded very confident.

Cooper swallowed and ran a hand across his sweating forehead. He threw a look at Hunter. The man sat immobile in his saddle, the shotgun returned to its back holster. His eyes were on McMurdo and Corday.

'No need for that, Mr McMurdo.'

'Won't be if'n you get offa EM property.'

'You got kinfolk of ours working as slaves in that mine. We want 'em, McMurdo,' a voice shouted from the posse.

'Who says so?' McMurdo put belligerence into his voice.

The Secret of Squaw Mountain

'I do.' Chad spoke for the first time.

'You letting a drifter talk for you, Sheriff?' Sarcasm laced McMurdo's voice.

'I ... I ...' The sheriff could find no words and Chad could see that the man was starting to come apart.

Chad dipped his head as though in resignation, but there was nothing resigned in the softly spoken words modulated to reach the man behind him. A tall, grizzled rancher who had lost two sons in a supposed Indian raid.

'Four men in the rocks to the right.'

'Seen 'em. Make your move.'

Chad liked the simplicity of the man. He lifted his head.

'The talking's over, McMurdo.' The Colt Frontiers that appeared by magic in Chad's hands spoke twice. Security guards either side of McMurdo and Corday dropped. It was the signal for all hell to break loose.

The lookouts on both corner towers opened up into the posse. Chad holstered a .45 and leapt from his horse, dragging the Winchester from its boot as the grizzled rancher, Coles by name, led half of the posse on a yelling charge towards the rocks. Chad snapped off two quick shots and the right-hand lookout tumbled from his perch, the top of his skull shot away, blood and brains leaking as he hit the ground. Chad moved to the protection of the doors, remembering the man on the canyon wall as they entered. He was up there now, crouched on one knee taking a bead on someone. Chad didn't give him a chance. He sighted quickly and squeezed gently on the trigger. The man threw up his arms and toppled forward, plunging down the face of the wall until he disappeared into the rocks at the bottom. Those who had not joined Coles on the charge, ran for the protection of the stockade wall. Two did not make it. Chad sent men either way along the wall to keep the men in the corner towers pinned down and stop them from picking off Coles and his group. Chad heard feet above. He tossed his rifle aside, drew the shotgun and stepped clear of the doorway, looking up. The shotgun exploded in his hands. A face looking down became an eyeless, crimson mask. The man accompanying him thought better of it and got off the platform.

As Coles and his men returned victorious, Tumbleweed sidled up to Chad, a stick of dynamite in his calloused hands. Somehow he had become part of the posse.

'Comes in a mite useful fer opening doors,' he cackled through his snowy beard, eyes sparkling in his seamed, weathered face.

Chad grinned back.

'A man with his heart in his work. Fire it up, Tumbleweed, just about there.' He indicated the ground where the two doors met and motioned everyone to retreat down the walls. The explosion, when it came, blew the doors open in a roaring cloud of smoke and dust and Chad went through

The Secret of Squaw Mountain 153

with it. He had reloaded the shotgun and as he emerged from the choking cloud, its thunderous double bark downed two men who were standing, gawping uncertainly in his direction. Coles led the rest of the posse in, concentrating fire power on the lookout positions, scoring deadly hits on three men. It was enough for the remainder of the demoralized security guards. One by one they threw down their weapons and raised their hands. Chad reloaded his shotgun once again, eyes ranging around the compound for McMurdo and Corday – who had vanished as soon as the shooting began. Coles took charge of rounding up the defeated guards.

'Where the hell's that damn sheriff?' he grumbled at Chad.

'Just checking the outside in case any tried to get away.' Sheriff Cooper hurried forward as he heard Coles' angry words. Chad and Coles exchanged glances.

'Appreciate it, Sheriff,' Chad said. 'Best you take some men into the mine and release the slaves. Take one of these guard gents to show you where.'

'I'll do that.' He had brightened considerably now that the shooting was over. 'Damn fine job men,' he called. 'I don't see McMurdo or Corday.' He glanced at Chad.

'You will,' Chad said softly. He had detected movement at the window of the office cabin though it was clear now. He stalked forward until he was within twenty feet of the cabin, halted, raised the shotgun and fired. The window shattered into a million pieces. 'Got any more of that door-opener, Tumbleweed?' he called back to the ex-miner.

'Just the one, son.'

'Only need the one,' Chad said dryly. 'Be obliged if'n you'd fire it up and toss it through that window.'

Giving a gap-toothed chuckle Tumbleweed obliged. A second after the spluttering, red stick entered through the window, the door opened and McMurdo and Corday emerged at a run and threw themselves flat. Five seconds later a dull boom shook the cabin. It shivered like a hound-dog with fleas, then blew itself apart, the boom escalating to a roar as planks and boards separated in a huge fan.

Timber rained from the sky, clattering down around the two prone men. As the dust began to settle, the two rose shakily to their feet.

'You'll pay for this,' McMurdo blustered, white-faced, but his words carried no conviction. He was a beaten man.

A shout went up from the posse members who had remained outside as a line of ragged, half naked figures were led from the mine by a strutting Sheriff Cooper. They were like children seeing daylight for the first time. Some fell to their knees, crying. Coles let out a whoop of joy as he saw one of his lost sons. He ran to him, hugging the thin emaciated form.

'Frank, where's Frank?'

The youth's eyes filled wih tears.

'He didn't make it, Pa,' he said brokenly.

Coles' joy turned to anger as he released his son and stalked forward to halt at Chad's side, staring at McMurdo.

'You son of a bitch!' he spat through clenched teeth.

'OK, Jesse, the law'll take care of this,' Cooper said importantly.

'The hell it will,' Jesse Coles said, pulled his Colt and pumped two bullets into McMurdo.

McMurdo gave a scream as red blossomed on his shirt-front. He tried to stem the flow of blood with his hands. It gouted beween his fingers as he toppled face down in the dirt.

Corday raised his hands.

'I was only following orders,' he began.

Coles would have shot him, but Chad stayed his hand.

'This one's mine.'

'Sheriff!' There was alarm in Corday's voice.

'Hold it, Hunter.' Cooper stepped forward and his face went white as the barrel of Coles' handgun pressed hard under his chin.

'Stay outta this, Roy,' he said mildly.

'We got some unfinished business, Corday, ten years unfinished,' Chad called coldly. The shotgun was back in its holster.

'I'm not drawing against you, Hunter. If'n you

kill me it'll be murder. Ten years?' The import of Chad's words hit him. 'I don't know you.' His eyes narrowed.

'The folks in Abilene paid good money for your hide ten years ago. I guess it's time they got it.'

Corday had dropped his hands to his sides, face suddenly grey with fear.

'Who are you?' His voice was a tortured whisper. His eyes seemed to know the answer.

'They called me the Undertaker before I retired,' Chad said quietly. Corday's hand was still going for his gun when four bullets from Chad's Colt Frontiers opened up his chest, spun him in a spray of red and laid him hard on the dirt next to McMurdo. 'Guess I'm out of retirement now,' he murmured.

Much later, his Appaloosa retrieved from a corral at the mine, Chad stood outside the boarding-house in Grand Mesa strapping his bedroll to the cantle of his saddle. The professor, Cora, Tom and Amos looked on silently. Kate was bedbound from her ordeal.

The professor had earlier provided an explanation for the silent bear that the Navaho offered human sacrifices to.

'Who the original He-with-no-Voice was is still yet to be found out, but I think Grey Wolf just capitalized on the legend. He may have been responsible for damaging the animal's vocal chords in the first place, but it's more likely to have been the result of a fight the animal had with, say, a mountain lion or even one of its own kind. Whatever, Grey Wolf supplied its carnivorous appetite with those unfortunate to venture onto the mountain. Probably, in times of hardship, Grey Wolf even sacrificed his own people, thus keeping a legend alive and other Indians off the Squaw. Grey Wolf set himself up as the guardian of He-with-no-Voice and became a kind of god himself.'

Chad finished lashing his bedroll in place as Cora asked,

'Will you be back this way, Chad? Pa's decided that Grand Mesa is as good a place as any to live, now he's found his lost city.'

'Reckon I'll be around from time to time,' Chad replied as he swung astride the Appaloosa.

'You still owe me a meal, brother,' Tom called out.

'Next time around,' Chad promised.

'What will you do now, Chad?' Amos asked.

'Got a little business with an Indian trader by the name of Beau Trasker to take care of.'

'Well don't stay away too long. A body gets lonely,' Cora said coyly.

Chad felt a hot flush burn over his body. He touched the brim of his hat.

'You can bet on it,' he breathed and turned the Appaloosa's head south.